HYPNOEROTICA

HYPNOEROTICA

Athena Michaels

First published in 2016 by Telos Publishing,
5A Church Road, Shortlands, Bromley, Kent
BR2 0HP, United Kingdom.

www.telos.co.uk

Hypnoerotica © 2016 Athena Michaels

ISBN: 978-1-84583-950-5

The moral right of the author has been asserted.

A catalogue record for this book is available from the British Library.

This book is sold subject to the condition that it shall not by way of trade or otherwise, be lent, resold, hired out or otherwise circulated without the publisher's prior written consent in any form of binding or cover other than that in which it is published and without a similar condition including this condition being imposed on the subsequent purchaser.

1
The Hypnotist

'And when I click my fingers, you will be wearing boots made of lead!'

The hypnotist on the stage stepped back with a flourish and snapped his fingers.

The man standing beside him started to stomp around the stage like Frankenstein's monster, his feet heavy and leaden, as the assembled audience laughed their appreciation.

Dave Toner loved doing his hypnosis magic show. It was a passion that he had fallen into at a young age after watching some incredible feats on television. With the internet to help him, he had read up as much as he could about mesmerism and magic, so that now, by the age of 25, he had become pretty accomplished in both.

It was a good way to earn a few extra pounds, too. Rather than sitting around at home with only his cat for company, he now got to go out, entertain people, get bought free drinks, get paid – and, more often than not, score with a gorgeous girl or bored housewife into the bargain.

Dave was not hesitant about using his powers for fun, as well ... Most of it was suggestion, aided by a knowledge of how the mind worked; but added to that, he had developed a very seductive speaking style. It lured people in, and before they knew it, he was inside their heads, and they were doing pretty much whatever he suggested.

It hadn't taken him long to realise that this ability could be used in many ways: like persuading women that they really liked him. That he was the best thing that had ever happened to them. If that involved them sucking his dick until he came, or cumming repeatedly themselves as he fucked them ... well, he had no complaints either way, and he saw no harm in it either, because he always made sure the woman had a good time too, and that she remembered nothing afterwards.

The one thing he didn't have was a steady girlfriend. But life was too short and too full of amazing sexual conquests for that to really trouble him. Plenty of time for that in the future, if he ever wanted it. For now, it was far more fun just having casual sex with hypnotised strangers. It left him free to live his life without the complication of a relationship to worry about.

What Dave didn't admit to himself was that this behaviour was somewhat addictive. And it never occurred to him that it was inappropriate or wrong and that he should stop.

Now, Dave scanned the crowd as his subject of the evening completed a stomping circuit of the stage.

He was looking for someone to keep him company later on ... and he thought he had found the perfect girl. She was sitting with a bloke at a table near the front of the stage. She was pretty, in a homely sort of way, with blonde curly hair held back with an Alice band, and a sensible sweater on over what looked like a simple cotton party dress. Very sensible.

But then, often the quiet-looking ones were the wildest in the sack ...

He spent a few moments releasing the man from his trance – ensuring that he was fully awake, with all triggers removed – and then sent him back to his seat, to another round of applause.

At another table near the back, a woman called out: 'Rubbish!'

Dave frowned momentarily. The group around that table had been heckling him all evening. It was five women in their early twenties, presumably out on some party night, and they were all fairly drunk. They had shouted out before, breaking his concentration, and had constantly moved around, going to the toilet, or to the bar for more cocktails, all during his act! They were very annoying and distracting.

Dave was getting pretty fed up with them. He could usually handle hecklers, but these women were loud and brash and seemed to have no interest whatsoever in his show.

He put them to the back of his mind, and announced that he was now in need of another assistant on stage.

His eyes scanned the crowd, pretending to consider who to pick. A dozen arms were being waved enthusiastically in the air, but Dave headed down into the crowd and made his way to the table where the blonde girl was sitting.

She was looking shyly at him, and then down at her lap, as the man she was sitting with grasped a bottle of Bud and lifted it to his lips to take a swig.

'What about you?' Dave asked gently.

She lifted her eyes to his, and he gave a little *push*.

She smiled and hesitated.

'I think the lady needs some encouragement,' said Dave in a practised way, and the audience applauded as he took her hand and led her out from the table and up onto the stage.

The man that had been sitting beside her called out, 'Go on, love,' and she looked back and smiled at him.

That's it, thought Dave. *Step one complete. Now for step two.*

On stage, he asked the woman what her name was.

'Sally,' came the timid reply.

He could have guessed that she would be a Sally ... she just had that look about her.

'What do you do?'

'I'm a receptionist.'

Again, he could have predicted the response.

'Okay, Sally,' he said, smiling reassuringly at her. 'I want you to sit in this chair here.'

He pulled out a chair and positioned it so that it was facing away from the audience. She sat down, facing the rear curtain of the theatre.

Dave turned to the crowd.

'Thank you ... thank you. Now. While I hypnotise Sally here, can I have complete silence, please? It's very important that nothing distracts us.'

'Get yer kit off!' shouted one of the women at the rear table. The crowd laughed, and Dave joined in ... all the better to keep them under some sort of control.

'Maybe later ...' He smiled out at them. 'Now then ... quiet please.'

Dave turned back to Sally, who was sitting rigidly in the chair. She was scared, he could tell, but that was fine; they all were at first.

He flicked off his stage microphone, as he didn't want

anyone to hear the induction; it could be very awkward if some of the crowd fell under his spell as well as young Sally here.

'Hi Sally,' he started. 'Everything's going to be completely fine. I just need you to take a deep breath in. That's right. And out. And another ... Good. Now then, just look into my eyes ...'

Dave took Sally through a standard induction, which took about two minutes. The crowd was quiet, and this allowed him to take Sally from being totally aware and in control, to a relaxed puddle of helpless femininity sitting on the chair in front of him.

When he had finished, she had her eyes closed and a happy smile on her lips, and her arms were loose and floppy at her sides.

When he was sure she was completely under, he turned back to the crowd.

'Sally is now ready,' he announced. 'But before we have her perform for us, just one final check.'

Dave switched off his mic again, and crouched down next to Sally.

'Open your eyes', he said.

Sally opened her eyes.

'Look deeply into my eyes,'

Sally obeyed.

Dave could tell that she was very deeply under his control.

'Sally, listen very carefully. When I say the words "love puppet", you will instantly return to this deeply hypnotised state. You love feeling as you are right now, and when I say "love puppet", you will return to this state, and you will obey all my commands. Do you understand?'

Sally, continuing to look unblinkingly into Dave's

eyes, murmured 'I understand', and Dave's cock jerked in his trousers. He was going to have fun with this one later!

Now then; on with the show.

Dave switched his mic back on, and turned back to the crowd.

'So now we need to find out something about Sally. Can you stand, my dear?'

Sally stood up and remained motionless.

'It's all right, Sally,' said Dave. 'You can move and talk now.'

The life returned to Sally, as though a switch had been pressed. She was back to normal – at least, what Dave thought was normal. A little shy, but clearly not hypnotised, and enjoying herself. Indeed, this was how he had instructed her to act during the induction.

Dave grinned at the audience and proceeded to take Sally through a typical day, but a day in which she had to pretend to ride a bicycle against a wind, rescue frogs and toads from the road in front of her, dance with a group of passing ballerinas, and then catch sight of her favourite actor sunbathing ... at which point she became very hot and bothered, and Dave only just stopped her from ripping all her clothes off there and then ... Then he had her dancing with a floor mop, thinking it was the actor, and finally giving the mop a passionate goodnight kiss ...

It was all good, crowd-pleasing stuff, and even the man sitting at Sally's table seemed happy, clapping and laughing and whooping along with her antics.

She was a great subject, and Dave's cock throbbed with the thought of what he would get up to later, after the show.

As the crowd's applause died down, Dave suggested

that Sally would stand to attention every time he tapped his foot. He then got her to sit down to put her (imaginary) shoes back on. And every time he tapped his foot, she leapt up and stood to attention, not quite knowing why.

The audience loved it, and clapped and cheered … all except for the small party of women at the back table, who started booing and catcalling. Dave frowned. He'd never known such a badly-behaved bunch of women.

As the act came to a close, so Dave sat Sally back down and removed all of the suggestions and triggers he had used on stage. She was a great subject, and she slipped back into a deep sleep with little prompting.

Once he had removed all but his prior instruction about returning into his power, Dave mentally double-checked that had not forgotten anything. He had read and, indeed, seen hypnotists who had been less diligent about removing all their triggers – something that could cause issues for the subjects for years to come. Dave wanted none of that, nor any of the hassle that law suits could bring if the affected parties ever realised what was happening, so he was as careful as he could be.

Sally was sitting down on the chair, back to the audience again, completely de-programmed apart from the instruction to wake.

'When I click my fingers, Sally, you will wake up,' he told her in his smooth, hypnotic voice. 'You will feel fine, as though you have just awakened from a deep, relaxing sleep, and you won't remember any of what has happened on this stage. But you will remember that you can return to this relaxed and happy state whenever I say the words "love puppet".'

Dave looked at the beautiful girl sitting relaxed in front of him and smiled.

He clicked his fingers, and Sally yawned, opened her eyes and stretched her arms. She blinked, and smiled at Dave. She seemed perfectly fine.

Now the test.

'Sally,' said Dave.

Sally cocked her head and looked up at him.

'You want to be my love puppet,' he said.

Dave watched with satisfaction as Sally's eyes blanked over and her face went slack. She drifted quickly back down into deep hypnosis, a slight smile on her face as she experienced the pleasurable feeling that Dave had told her she would find there.

Dave's cock leapt again.

'And now you will wake again, with no memory of the last few minutes, but you will find you need to come to my dressing room after the show. I have something for you. You will find an excuse to come alone.'

'I understand. Alone,' whispered Sally, deep in her trance.

Dave smiled. Excellent. 'And now, Sally, when I click my fingers, you will wake again, relaxed and happy.'

He snapped his fingers, and the life returned to Sally's face, and she grinned and stretched once more.

Dave switched his microphone back on, turned to the audience and asked for a big round of applause for Sally.

The audience – all except the women at the back – started clapping wildly, and Sally shyly gave a curtsey as Dave helped her down off the stage and back to her table. The man there was by now very drunk, and he just smiled at her, slapping her bottom as she went to sit back down in her chair. As Dave turned back to the stage, he saw the beginnings of an argument breaking out between them. All the better to further his cause, he thought.

Back on stage, Dave took his final bow, thanked the audience and headed backstage. As he went, he heard the booing and catcalling once more from the table of women at the back. What was their problem?

Ah well ... nothing he could do about that. Dave headed to his dressing room, and quickly checked that it was in good order. He kept it tidy for precisely this reason: his after-show liaisons. The bottle of champagne and two glasses were also in place, as was the comfy *chaise longue* with velvet throws and cushions all over it.

Dave smiled to himself, and adjusted his cock through his trousers. He had had a boner pretty much from the moment Sally had come up on stage, and it had become fairly uncomfortable for him. He wasn't a small man, and when his cock reached full size ... well ... there wasn't that much room in a pair of boxers and stage trousers.

There was a gentle rap on his dressing-room door, and Dave made a quick, final visual check before opening the door to find Sally standing there.

'Why hello, Sally,' Dave said, all smiles.

'Erm ... hi ...' Sally said, looking at the ground.

'So nice of you to come backstage.'

Sally blushed. 'I'm not sure why ... My boyfriend ... he got drunk and went off ... I ... It was ... I mean ...'

Dave took pity on her.

'That's fine, Sally. Come in.'

He held the door open and let Sally come past him into his dressing room. He slipped the DO NOT DISTURB sign into place on the other side of the door, and closed it behind her.

'You were excellent on stage tonight, Sally,' said Dave.

'Really?' Sally smiled shyly. She wasn't used to

getting compliments.

'Yes, really, really good. Couldn't you tell from the audience?'

Sally frowned. 'Well ... yes ... though I can't really remember ...' She laughed nervously. 'Something to do with a mop?'

Dave laughed. 'Yes indeed. A lot of men in that room were very jealous of that mop.' He went over to the champagne and started undoing the foil. 'Drink?'

'Oh ... I don't know,' said Sally. 'My boyfriend ... Maybe I shouldn't.'

Dave finished releasing the cork, and it popped with a satisfying burst. He filled the two glasses carefully with the champagne, then picked up one of the glasses and held it out to Sally.

'Go on ... just the one glass. Celebrate your success tonight.'

Sally smiled and accepted the glass. 'Okay then. Just the one ...'

Dave mimed a *Cheers*, and they clinked glasses and drank. It was good champagne; but then Dave always had the best.

'Please, have a seat,' said Dave, gesturing to the *chaise longue*. He himself sat on his make-up chair.

Sally sat down, her hand stroking the velvet of the throws on the bed-like chair. 'It's lovely,' she said.

Dave put down his glass. Enough of this. His cock was throbbing fit to burst, and the sight of Sally sitting there was turning him on immensely.

'Sally,' he said.

'Yes?' She looked at him all wide-eyed and friendly.

'I think ... I think you want to be my love puppet.'

At the words 'love puppet,' Sally's eyes widened in surprise, and then quickly drooped closed. Her face relaxed, and her hands, still holding the glass, dropped to her lap. Dave quickly retrieved the drink and placed it safely on the table. Then he turned his attention to his new conquest.

'Sally, can you hear me?'

Sally nodded slowly.

'You can speak,' said Dave.

'Yes, I hear you,' said Sally in a slow monotone.

Dave smiled in satisfaction. Just a few checks, and then he could have some fun!

'Sally, can you tell me, have you had sex before?'

He had a code of honour about this. If she was still a virgin, he'd be sending her away as soon as possible. He didn't like that kind of responsibility.

'Yes.'

'And how old are you, Sally?'

'I'm 23.'

'Who was the man at your table tonight?'

'He was my boyfriend.'

'How do you feel about him?'

'He's okay. We fight a lot. He drinks too much sometimes ...'

Dave nodded to himself. Such a shame that there were jerks around who didn't know when they had it good. She was a sweet girl. He liked her. Well, as much as he would allow himself to like anyone, that is.

'Sally. Listen to me carefully. Listen to my voice. When you hear me speak to you, then you will obey.'

'I will obey.'

It always gave Dave such a thrill to hear those words coming from a pretty girl.

'Sally, it's very warm in here. You are comfortable. But you are also feeling very sexy. Very sexy and horny.'

Sally started to squirm gently on the *chaise longue*. Her

eyes were still closed, but her pink tongue dipped out and licked her lips.

'When you look at me, you will see the most amazing lover in the world. A man you desire. One you will do anything for. Do you understand?'

'Yes. I understand.'

'So, open your eyes, Sally, and then do what you need to do for release.'

Sally opened her eyes and momentarily looked around in confusion. Then her gaze alighted on Dave, and he saw her pupils instantly dilate in sexual arousal. She smiled at him and shuffled gently on the seat.

'Why are you sitting over there?' she asked.

Dave smiled at her. 'That's a good question ...' He was pleased at how receptive she was, and liked the look of adoration in her expression.

He shifted and sat next to her on the seat. Sally put her hand on his leg and stroked it gently. 'I've always liked you,' she said.

Dave put one arm around her shoulders, and smiled at her. 'I've always liked you too,' he said, moving closer to her, and kissing her gently on the lips. Even though they had only just met, his voice was sincere. He never invited anyone back that he didn't like, after all.

Sally responded by snaking her other hand around his neck and pulling him into a passionate kiss, which seemed to go on forever. Her tongue snaked out again and explored Dave's own lips and tongue, engaging in a gentle and very erotic dance with him. Then she pulled back, breathing heavily.

'It's rather warm in here, isn't it,' she said, looking directly into Dave's eyes.

'It is, rather,' he replied.

'Let me,' said Sally, dropping to her knees in front of

him. She reached up and pulled off the bow tie he was wearing, and then unbuttoned his shirt. Once it was undone, she helped him slide it off his arms, leaving him bare-chested.

Sally moved closer and kissed his chest, her hands moving over him, her fingers gently stroking and tweaking his nipples.

Dave shuddered in pleasure. Feeling him sigh, Sally locked her lips onto one of his nipples, flicking it with her tongue and gently wetting it with her saliva.

She pulled away and started to undo his trousers, pulling the zipper down. Dave helped by raising his bottom off the chair and allowing her to pull his trousers and underpants down. They hung around his ankles for a moment, and then Sally pulled them free.

His cock emerged into the air, and bounced as Sally removed the constricting clothing.

She reached out her hand and gently ran a finger over his length. He was big, but not too big. Sally decided that he was just right for her.

'Can I …? May I …?' she asked, looking up into Dave's eyes.

He smiled and nodded. 'I'd be offended if you didn't!' he said, and then gasped as she grasped the shaft of his penis and gently squeezed it while stroking it up and down.

She brought the purple head to her lips and kissed it gently, before opening her mouth and allowing his cock to enter her.

Dave shuddered again as the sensation of Sally's lips and tongue on his engorged cock travelled up and down his body.

She sucked like her life depended on it. She teased the sensitive spot just below the glans with her tongue, while using her hands to stroke and rub the shaft, and her nails to gently manipulate his balls. It was exquisite pleasure.

Dave could tell that Sally was getting into this really well. He hadn't had to give her any suggestions yet. He guessed that she must have been really frustrated with her boyfriend.

She licked up and down his shaft and sucked at his balls while gently stroking her hand up and down his length. She was amazing at this!

'Sally,' said Dave. 'You need to take your clothes off for me now ...'

Sally looked up at him and nodded, reluctantly releasing his cock and standing before him.

She slowly started to strip.

First the sweater, which came up and off her body.

Then she reached behind her, making her breasts press against the fabric of her dress, and unzipped the back of the garment. She shimmied it down her body until it pooled at her feet.

Underneath, she was wearing matching powder blue bra and panties.

Dave looked at her body. Very nice. She was slim but not skinny; her waist pulled in nicely and her hips flared. Her panties clung to her mound, and her ass was nice and rounded. Very nice indeed.

Sally continued to take off her bra, releasing her breasts to bounce in front of her. They were a lovely size, not too small, and the nipples were hard and erect, testament to how turned on the girl was right now.

Finally, she hooked her thumbs into her panties and slipped them off, revealing a neatly-trimmed bush of blonde hair matching that on her head.

Dave grinned. 'Very good, Sally ...' He kicked the

clothing at his feet away into a corner. Then he pulled off his socks.

Sally, he noticed, was still very taken with his cock, and kept her hand on it, stroking it gently.

At a word from him, she fell to her knees and sucked him deeply into her hot mouth. Dave shuddered, feeling his knees tremble. He was going to have to take control of this situation before she had him cumming before his time!

'Sally,' he ordered. 'Lie on the couch.'

Sally stood and obeyed, draping herself on the couch in a very seductive manner.

It was now Dave's turn to kneel before her, and to stroke and pleasure her pussy. He ran his nails gently through her hair, and rubbed his thumb against her clitoris. This elicited moans of pleasure from the girl, and she opened her legs wider to allow him better access.

When he thought she was ready, Dave stood and positioned his cock just outside the entrance to her vagina.

Sally had her eyes closed, and her hands were clenched, awaiting the final act. Dave gently stroked her hair, and asked her to open her eyes.

She obeyed and looked up into Dave's own eyes. His hypnotic stare pinned her, and he saw all trace of resistance disappear from her face, leaving just obedience and a yearning for him to take her.

'As I enter you, Sally,' Dave instructed, 'you will start to orgasm. And every five strokes, you will cum again, stronger than before ... This will continue until I cum myself.'

Sally breathed in anticipation.

'Do you understand?'

'Yes,' she gasped.

And Dave slowly slid his cock deep into her pussy.

The moment he was fully embedded, he felt Sally shudder as the first of her many orgasms started. She moaned as he gently slid his cock almost all the way out again, and then back in.

He started to fuck her slowly, and on the fifth stroke in, Sally gasped as she came. He felt the walls of her cunt constrict around his cock, and then become hot and wet as the moisture flooded from her.

He picked up the pace.

On the tenth stroke she came again, harder this time.

Fifteenth and she was moaning.

Twentieth and she was thrashing her head back and forth, helplessly cumming over and over and over on his pistoning cock.

It was all getting too much for Dave, and he felt the pressure increase in his balls as he prepared for his own orgasm.

Sally was gasping and crying out now, cumming over and over, and Dave rammed his cock into her for a final time, erupting his seed into her and gasping as he came hard.

He stopped moving, and felt Sally's body jerking from orgasmic aftershocks as she came down from her high.

His breathing steadied, and he pulled from her with a satisfying plop, her stretched pussy returning to normal after the immense pounding it had taken.

Sally had her eyes closed and a big smile on her face as she too recovered. Dave grinned to himself. It was always a pleasure to service his audience … and he liked to leave them happy and wanting more.

Dave located his clothes and started pulling them back on.

'Sally,' he said. 'You need to put your clothes back on again now.'

Sally stood and did just that, replacing her panties and bra, slipping her dress back on, and picking up her cardigan.

Dave, ever the gentleman, reached behind her and zipped up the dress, keeping her blonde hair out the way of the zipper.

Sally now stood there, a marionette with broken strings.

Dave felt momentarily sorry for her, but pushed the thought away. *Naaa.*

'Sally,' he said. 'I have some more instructions for you ...'

He got her to open her eyes and gaze deeply into his again, ensuring that she was fully under his influence. He strengthened his control over her, taking her through deeper and deeper relaxation, until he was certain she was completely his to command.

The sight of this gorgeous woman, whom he had just fucked comprehensively, standing before him, eyes wide and in an unbreakable trance, aroused Dave like nothing else.

He instructed her to think that she had dreamed the liaison she had just enjoyed, but to remember the dream as being amazing. She was not to discuss it with her boyfriend at all. And when she felt she needed the release of uninhibited sex again, she was to seek Dave out and attend another of his shows.

Other than that, she was to continue with her normal life, to please her boyfriend as far as she could, and to be happy and relaxed about everything that she dreamed had happened.

Sally confirmed her agreement with everything that

Dave had said, and the final thing he did was to get her mobile number from her. You never knew ...

There was suddenly a rapping at the door.

'Dave? Dave Toner?' said a voice. 'There's a chap here wants a word.'

Dave frowned. *What now?*

He finished off with Sally. 'When I snap my fingers, you will wake and remember only that we had champagne in my room. You wanted to congratulate me on the great show tonight.'

He clicked his fingers as the door opened, revealing the theatre manager, and behind him, Sally's boyfriend.

'What's going on here?' said the boyfriend. 'Sally?'

'Oh, hi Pete,' said Sally, having snapped into life the moment Dave clicked his fingers. 'Sorry I was so long. I wanted to thank Dave here for the show tonight. Well, as I seemed to be the star, it seemed the right thing to do. We had champagne!'

She gestured to the bottle and glasses.

'I hope you don't mind,' Dave said. 'She came to the room and ... well, it seemed the right thing to do.'

Pete scowled at Dave, and then at Sally. 'I guess so,' he growled.

'Oh, Pete,' admonished Sally, brighter and happier now than she had been before or even during the show. 'Dave has been a perfect gentleman. I might even come back and enjoy watching him again!'

Dave smiled at that. Clearly his commands had taken well ... She would be back for a second helping ...

'Well, thanks again, Dave,' Sally breezed, 'See you!' And, grabbing Pete by the arm, she headed off.

The theatre manager watched them go. 'Pretty girl,' he mused, shooting Dave a look.

'Indeed,' Dave said. 'Nice to have someone to share a

drink with after the show.'

The manager nodded. 'Not so good for you, though,' he said.

'What do you mean?'

'We've had a complaint.'

'A complaint? Who from? What about?'

'Them girls at the back table. They claim you didn't do the act as advertised. That it was all fake, and that you insulted them.'

'I *what?*' Dave was incredulous. This had never happened before. Sure, there were people who didn't believe, who thought it was all done with stooges and fixed, but they just kept their scepticism to themselves. They didn't complain.

The manager nodded. 'Afraid so. And one of them is married to the Mayor, so I can't be seen not to be doing anything about it, or he'll close this place down! You know our licence is up for renewal.'

'So what are you going to do?'

The manager hesitated. 'You know I like your act, Dave, and it does well … but …'

'But what?'

'But I'm going to have to let you go.'

'What?'

'Yeah. Sorry. But that's the way it is.'

'Sorry?' Dave was amazed.

'Yeah. Tonight's going to have to be your last performance. After the weekend we have some singers who can fill in until we find another cabaret-type thing to keep the punters happy.'

Dave's face fell. He knew this was bullshit and he was being made a scapegoat. It was so unfair!

'Nothing I can do,' said the manager. 'I'll have tonight's payment for you at the office when you go.

Thanks for everything.'

The manager turned and left Dave's dressing room. Dave watched him go, anger seething in his stomach. How could they do this to him? He had purposely kept away from that table, ignored all of their insults, because he had suspected they were trouble. Where was the justice in this? It just wasn't right!

He would have to do something in return. Those bitches couldn't get away with this!

He considered the situation. The Mayor's wife, eh …? But who were the other women? How could he find out?

Dave smiled to himself. He had a fair bit of money put aside. He could afford to take a couple of months off and enjoy himself … and he intended to enjoy himself for certain … with those bitches who had lied about him. It could have stood it if he'd been taking the rap for something he'd actually done, like shagging his pretty victims, but to be blamed for something he hadn't done at all was another thing entirely.

He pulled on his jacket and packed his things into his overnight case. Luckily his act didn't need anything special in the way of props, so there was never much in his dressing room.

On his way out he picked up his money at the box office and bade a cheery farewell to the manager, who lurked embarrassed at the back.

The manager didn't know it, but he had done Dave a favour. He was going to start using his talents in an even better, more exciting way. And those women, whoever they were, would all pay for their part in his dismissal. Then he would find a way to get his job back. Even if it meant hypnotising the manager! But not yet – that would be just too easy.

Whistling, Dave headed out to his car and home.

Tomorrow was another day, and with some planning, he would be ready to teach those women a lesson they probably wouldn't ... but then he might let them ... remember. After all, that would be a much better idea than just shagging them and making them forget. He could in fact allow them to remember, and crave him again and again ... Oh, the thought of sweet revenge – and hopefully some very good sex.

2
Anthea

The next day, Dave started planning.

A local paper furnished him with the information he was after. That the Mayor would be visiting a shopping centre the following weekend, along with his wife Anthea, to open a new store.

So she was called Anthea.

Some internet research called up other facts and some pictures of the woman, and indeed he recognised her from that rowdy table the other night. She was 24 years old. And obviously a trophy wife, as the Mayor was pushing 40!

Dave had thought long and hard about what she and her friends had done, and he really couldn't understand it. But he was going to have payback. What he really needed though was someone to help him.

Sally was at home, finishing off the washing up. Her boyfriend was out working, and she would have been working herself except that this happened to be a half-day for her. So she occupied herself with cleaning and tidying the house, as well as a little afternoon television. It was somewhat mind-numbing, but she didn't mind.

Sally's mobile phone buzzed, and she idly looked at the UNKNOWN NUMBER message before answering. It was probably someone from work trying to get hold of her.

'Hello?'

The voice on the other end was male. 'Hi, is Pete there?'

'Oh, I'm sorry, he's at work at the moment. Can I take a message?'

'Love puppet. Keep the phone to your ear.'

Sally's eyes opened wide and glazed over. The arm not holding the phone relaxed and fell to her side and a gentle smile came to her mouth. She felt a wave of pleasure rush over her, tingling her nerve endings.

'Can you hear me, Sally?'

'Yes, I can hear you.'

'In future, the words "love puppet" will affect you only if you are on your own. Otherwise you will apologise, say "There's no-one here by that name," and then hang up. It will be a wrong number. Do you understand?'

'I understand.'

'That's excellent, Sally. Now here is what I want you to do ...'

The following weekend, the local shopping arcade was buzzing. The Mayor was visiting to open a new branch of Kebabs-R-Us, the popular fast food chain, and there were free samples and drinks and all sorts being offered to the public to gain their interest. There was even a brass band from the local Rotary Club!

The Mayor, Peter Mackie, was resplendent in his chain of office. He had arrived in one of his fleet of limousines, and had been ushered with his wife to the back of the new shop to meet the owners and staff. In a few minutes' time he would cut the proverbial red ribbon at the front, thus signalling that the store was now open for business.

There was a small crowd assembling at the front of the shop, where the ribbon had been mounted between two free-standing posts, ready for the Mayor's scissors.

Dave Toner was standing a little down the mall from the shop, watching the proceedings with interest. It wouldn't be long now ...

After a little waiting, there was a small commotion, and the Mayor and his wife, Anthea, emerged from the front of the shop, smiling at everyone.

Anthea was wearing a conservative pants suit in cream, and looked very stylish indeed. Dave recognised her immediately. She was certainly the right woman.

Peter Mackie said a few words about kebabs and cracked a joke, at which everyone laughed politely, and then declared the shop open.

He cut the ribbon, and the two halves fell aside, allowing the first customers inside.

As Dave had suspected they would, the Mayor and his wife stayed outside, chatting to people as they thronged to take advantage of the opening day offers and free tasters.

Dave watched Anthea intently. She was standing to one side, slightly embarrassed at what was going on, while her husband pressed palms with anyone and everyone he could.

At that moment, there was a cry from across the mall,

and a girl in tight silver hotpants and a loose T-shirt skidded out from one of the other shops on roller skates. She careered across the mall, and crashed headlong into Anthea, knocking her to the ground! Dave was moving as soon as he saw her. He pushed past everyone, and got to Anthea first. He helped her back to her feet, and then, with a protective arm around her shoulders, ushered her over to a nearby bench.

Behind him, Sally got herself back on her feet again, and with a smile of apology, roller-skated off down the mall, vanishing into the distance.

Sitting on the seat with Anthea, Dave feigned concern. He quickly checked that she was indeed all right, and then launched straight into a fast induction.

Sometimes known as the handshake induction, the technique was perfected by psychiatrist Milton H Erickson. It confuses the reception centres of the brain, and makes the subject enter a fugue state very quickly indeed. Dave made to shake Anthea's hand, but didn't, and instead manipulated her hand and wrist, slipping her into a trance. With some smooth, gentle words, she collapsed into sleep almost immediately.

'You can still hear my voice, Anthea,' he said quickly, as he didn't have much time. 'But you will not hear or listen to anyone else, only to my voice. Listening to me makes you feel good, and when you feel good, you are happy to do what I say.'

Dave glanced up and around. The crowd around the kebab shop were realising what had happened, and someone was informing the Mayor.

'You are happy to obey me, Andrea. You want to obey me as it makes you feel good.'

Andrea moaned gently in response. Excellent.

'Now, when I say the words "love puppet", you will

return to this state with no further prompting from me. When I say "love puppet" you will listen to my voice and obey me. Do you understand, Anthea?'

'I understand,' came the slow response.

'I'll count to three, and when I reach three, you will wake, groggy, and with no memory of our discussion. But you will remember my command and act on it.'

Dave looked up. The Mayor was striding over toward him with a concerned look on his face.

'One. Two. Three.'

Anthea stirred and opened her eyes. She was a little groggy, and when her husband arrived, she looked up at him and blinked.

'Are you okay darling?' he asked.

'I'm … I'm fine …' Anthea said, shaking her head a little. 'Nothing broken, anyway.'

'I'm trained in first aid,' said Dave helpfully. 'I think she's fine, just a little shaken.'

'Thank you,' said the Mayor. 'That's very kind of you.'

Anthea stood up with some assistance from Peter, and got her balance. 'I'm fine. Really I am.'

'Who was that crazy girl on the skates?' asked the Mayor. 'Where did she go?'

Some of the people looking on shrugged and stared around as though she was still in sight.

'Come on,' he said to Anthea. 'Let's get you a nice cup of tea.' He turned back to Dave. 'And thank you again for your help.'

'That's fine,' Dave replied, smiling broadly. 'It was nothing.'

Dave watched as the Mayor led his wife off to the kebab shop for a cup of England's finest. He had planted his seed. Now he needed to ensure it was firmly embedded, and to take advantage of this up-herself wife and her friends. He smiled again, thinking of the fun that he was going to have.

In his trousers, his cock jerked as he conjured up some special scenarios he was certain all parties would enjoy. Well ... maybe not the Mayor ... but that wasn't really Dave's problem, was it? Dave walked away, enjoying the arousal that this first step to revenge gave him. This was going to be fun!

The next day saw Dave sitting in his car outside Peter and Anthea Mackie's home. He was waiting for the Mayor to head off, leaving his wife alone.

While he waited, Dave listened to the radio, occasionally humming along to the songs and generally enjoying himself.

Eventually, the door to the house opened, and the Mayor emerged. He was dressed for the office, and carrying a small holdall. He bade farewell to his wife, and headed down the drive to his own car. After a moment, he pulled away and disappeared down the street.

Dave waited five minutes, just in case the man had forgotten something and returned. When he didn't reappear, Dave left his own car and sauntered up to the front door.

He rang the bell and waited.

After a moment, the door opened, and Anthea was there. She was wearing a rather fetching velvet tracksuit, the sort of designer-wear that was all the rage among the well-heeled.

She looked Dave up and down and frowned. He knew that she recognised him but couldn't place him.

'Yes?' she asked. 'Can I help you?'

Dave grinned. 'I think you can. Love puppet.'

Anthea looked at him and started to say, 'What do you mean ...', but then her eyes drooped, unable to resist the post-hypnotic suggestion that he had placed on her.

Her hand fell from the door, and she stood there in the doorway with her eyes closed, head bowed and arms limp.

Dave quickly checked outside. No-one was watching or passing.

'Is there anyone else in the house with you?' he asked.

Anthea shook her head. 'No.'

Dave took her by the hand and entered the house, shutting the door behind them. Then he led Anthea through the house and into the living room.

'Sit down, Anthea,' he commanded.

The woman obediently sat on one of the chairs. Her eyes were still closed.

Dave sat beside her and picked up one of her hands. Her arm was loose. It fell back into her lap when he released it.

'Anthea,' Dave began, 'I want you to listen to my voice. Can you hear me?'

Anthea nodded.

'Open your eyes.'

Anthea opened her eyes. She was a little confused, but found herself looking directly into Dave's eyes. They were grey with flecks of green, and the green seemed to pick up and reflect the light.

Anthea was aware that Dave was speaking to her, though not of what he was saying. She was drifting on a very pleasurable cloud of happiness. She was content and very, very happy.

Dave worked on her for twenty minutes, deepening

her trance and implanting several commands in her subconscious. By the time he had finished, he knew that she was his. Completely and utterly. Mind and body.

While he spoke gently to her, he continued to emphasise his will over hers. How she must obey him.

She smiled and confirmed every new implanted command. She was so easy to control. Dave chuckled to himself and congratulated himself on finding such a good subject.

Someone rang the doorbell while he was programming Anthea, but she completely ignored it. She had been told to respond only to Dave's voice. Anything else she simply didn't hear.

When he had finished, she sat on the chair, eyes open, looking at nothing. Her face was relaxed and her mouth slightly open. Her hands were folded in her lap, again, very relaxed.

She was, Dave noted, very pretty. Her blonde hair was in a style a little like that Farrah Fawcett had popularised a couple of decades before, and she wore little make-up, but what she did wear emphasised her eyes and lips.

She had pert breasts, and lovely legs, albeit hidden under the blue velvet of her track suit. Dave couldn't wait to see more. How the Mayor had managed to land such a stunning woman was beyond him. He guessed it must be the money … or the position of power on the Council. Whichever it was, he was one lucky son of a bitch. But now Dave was too!

'Stand up, Anthea.'

Anthea did as she was commanded. In this state, she could do nothing else. Dave had done an exceptionally good job on her.

'Turn around for me.'

Anthea slowly turned on the spot, and Dave could see that her bum was perfectly hugged by the tight material of the tracksuit bottoms. She was lovely.

'Stop.'

Dave stood and inspected his new conquest. She was about five feet tall and slim, her hair was blonde and cascaded down her back ... She was gorgeous.

'Anthea, you will now undress slowly for me.'

Anthea started to remove her tracksuit top, but her face was relaxed still, showing no emotions.

'Stop.' Dave needed to do something about the robotic stiltedness of her movements. 'Anthea, you are with your lover. You want to seduce him. As you remove your clothes, you will become more and more aroused. With each item of clothing you remove, your arousal will increase.'

It was a weird quirk, but he didn't enjoy it if the woman didn't. He couldn't understand why, but it was something in his psychology. Yes, he liked them to worship him, but it was only fair that they had a really good time as well.

The change in Anthea was startling. Gone was the good little housewife, and in her place a steamy seductress. She looked at Dave, and there was a spark of passion in her eyes. Her lips pursed, and she gently took her bottom lip between her teeth as she regarded Dave as a shark might regard its next meal.

She started moving, very sexy and slow, and removed her track suit top. Underneath she was wearing a simple T-shirt, and no bra. Dave could see that under the material her nipples were erect from excitement.

The T-shirt was next to come off, and her breasts were revealed. They were full and round, and her nipples were like cigar butts. He loved them and wanted to suck them until they grew even harder, but he resisted while she completed her task of removing her clothing.

She reached down and slid off her tracksuit bottoms. She was wearing a simple lace thong underneath, nothing fancy, but it fitted her as though it had been painted on.

She pulled her slim legs out from the trousers and placed them with the top on the sofa.

Then she fell to her knees in front of Dave, and started to help him remove his clothing too. Dave hadn't asked her to do this, but he noted that he had told her that she was with her lover – well, that was soon to be true – and her own imagination had filled in the blanks as to how she should behave.

Dave helped her, and soon he was naked too. He reached down and cupped Anthea's chin in his hand, raising her head. He gazed into her eyes, and smiled with pleasure at the way she locked onto him, her mouth relaxing slightly as she slipped instantly into trance again.

'That's excellent, Anthea,' said Dave, and she smiled, pleased with the praise, as he had instructed her to be.

'Now, darling, we're going to head up to the bedroom, and you are going to make love to me, and it is going to be the most intense and passionate sex you have ever had. Far surpassing your husband, or any other lovers you might have had. I excite you. I thrill you. My touch makes you desire me more. You want me so badly …'

Dave watched as Andrea's face went through a myriad small changes as his commands took root. Her pupils dilated in lust, her smile widened, and she became eager to start.

Anthea grabbed hold of Dave's arm and all but dragged him up the stairs, although he just managed to scoop up his clothes on the way. The house was nice, and expensively furnished, and the bedroom she led him into had a nice big double bed. It was all white furniture and furnishings. Very clean looking.

Well, let's dirty this up, Dave thought.

Anthea pushed Dave back onto the bed, and before he could say a word, she had peeled off her panties and was crawling up the sheets toward him. She kissed his legs, up his groin, and in a single movement, engulfed his dick in her mouth. Her hands fluttered either side as she gently sucked and worshipped his cock. Dave lay back, arms behind his head, and enjoyed the sensation as she expertly sucked and caressed him, licking him up and down like a lollypop and then popping the head back in her mouth and suckling on him while caressing his shaft and teasing his balls with her perfectly manicured nails.

With her hand still on his cock, she kissed up his stomach and paused at his nipples to suck and tease them with her teeth, before kissing and nibbling on his neck, making his cock leap in her hand.

After a few moments of this, Anthea straddled Dave, and with one hand positioned his cock to enter her pussy. She was already damp, and she slid down easily, engulfing him deeply in her body, and emitting a small moan of pleasure as she did so.

She then started to rock gently on his cock, letting the shaft slide slowly in and out of her depths, while the topside of the shaft teased her clitoris.

Dave looked up at her face. Her eyes were closed in pleasure, and her mouth was slightly open. He was amazed at how tight she was around his cock. Tight and hot. This was one turned-on woman.

She started to rock slightly more vigorously, allowing more of his dick to slide out of her each time, before she plunged back onto it again. As she moved, so her rhythm picked up, and Dave rocked his hips in time with her thrusts. He stroked the sides of her waist, feeling her smooth skin. His hands moved up over her skin to cup her full breasts. He held them for a moment, letting his thumbs move over and around her big, erect nipples.

Her movements became greater still, and her breathing changed to be in time with them.

'Oh ... oh ... mm ... oh ... yes ... yes ...'

She was rapidly approaching her first orgasm, but in her excitement she moved a little too fast and his cock plopped out of her.

She moaned in frustration, losing her rhythm. Sliding her hand back between their bodies, she quickly positioned him again. Soon he was back deep inside her, as she started moving again, picking up the pre-orgasmic movements as before.

This time she didn't move too far, and her breathing and moans and sighs continued.

'Oh ... oh ... yes ... yes ... mm ... yes ... oh ... God ...'

She moved faster and faster and his dick plunged again and again into her.

'Yes ... yes ... God ... ooohhhhhhhhhh ...'

And she came all over his dick. Her body clamped on him, and she shuddered from head to feet as the orgasm washed over her. Her hands clenched the bedsheets, and her face constricted in pleasure.

Dave smiled again. The feelings coming from his cock were amazing. He wasn't ready to cum yet; but Anthea had cum, and how! She'd even done it without him telling her she should. She was incredible!

She collapsed on his body, smiling happily to herself. Dave pushed her off him and onto her back. Anthea smiled up at him.

'What are you doing, mister?' she asked.

'What do you think?' Dave replied.

He moved her legs apart and got into position.

With one thrust, he buried his cock into her pussy again, and she gasped with pleasure.

'Oh my God, you're so big!'

Dave started to thrust into her. Slowly at first, and then with harder and harder strokes until the bed was protesting and rocking rhythmically.

The headboard started to knock against the wall. Tap. Tap. Tap.

Let the neighbours make of that what they would! Anthea was in no position to protest. In fact she was not protesting at all, but cumming again as he thrust into her.

'Cummmmiiinnngggg!' she cried as her body shook again in the throes of pleasure.

Dave slowed a little to let her recover, then picked up his pace again.

He slid his hard cock all the way out, and then smoothly back in again so that she felt the whole length of him going inside her.

This drove her to a third orgasm, and this time she screamed so loudly that he was sure the neighbours must think she was being murdered or something.

As she moaned and sobbed and came down from the intense pleasure, Dave pulled out and stroked her body gently with his hand.

She was an amazing woman, and a superb lover.

Dave even thought she might be a keeper ... Time would tell.

She turned on her side and snuggled up to him in post-orgasmic bliss.

Dave stroked her hair as her eyes closed and she settled onto him.

Before she slept, however, he had to get some more information from her.

'Darling,' he said. 'Can you open your eyes for me?'

Anthea's eyes opened sleepily, and she looked up into his face, her smile only for him.

'Yes, sweetie?'

'Look into my eyes, darling.'

Anthea looked, and was immediately in trance again. Her breathing slowed, and her face relaxed, eyes wide open and staring into his.

'Can you tell me who the other girls were who were with you the other night at the club? At the hypnosis show?'

'Yes,' said Anthea. 'There was Charlie, Petra, Nikki and Kym.'

'Thank you. And do you have contact details for them?'

'I do.'

Dave made a mental note to obtain the details from Anthea as soon as he could. But first, there was some unfinished business to attend to.

He gently pushed Anthea over onto her back, and positioned himself over her again. Her hands automatically moved to his sides, and she caressed him gently.

She looked up into his eyes, half in trance and half with desire. She couldn't help herself.

Dave looked into her eyes. 'I'm going to make love to you again, darling, and when I start to cum, you will too. It will be the most fulfilling and amazing experience you have ever had. Do you understand?'

Anthea bit her bottom lip between her teeth and

nodded.

And then Dave started to make love to her again, plunging deeply into her. Anthea for her part rocked her hips and took him. She clenched against him, milking his cock as it thrust into her, and as they moved together, so their passion rose higher and higher until Dave felt the familiar gathering feeling in his balls, and knew that he was starting the inexorable road to his own release.

They moved faster and faster, Anthea's cunt sucking at his cock hungrily, her muscles rippling and teasing and stroking him, even as he was stroking her insides.

And then they were both cumming at the same time. Dave felt his dick expand, and start to pump load after load of hot semen into her willing and spasming pussy. Anthea, feeling him expand, started to cum again herself, the electricity shooting over her whole body, making her jerk and twitch as she shared Dave's orgasm. Her cunt squeezed and clenched, and it brought Dave harder in an extended orgasm. It was unbelievable.

As they came down from the intense explosion, Dave pulled out slightly, and then thrust back in deeply. The head of his cock brushed against Anthea's cervix, and the deep sensation made her cum again, helplessly moaning and thrashing against Dave's cock.

'That's the way to do it,' thought Dave with satisfaction.

He pulled out and got off the bed.

As he dressed, Anthea watched him sleepily from the bed. She was totally fulfilled and very satisfied.

When he was dressed, Dave bent over her and kissed her on the forehead.

'Until next time,' he said.

Anthea smiled up at him and snaked an arm around his neck, pulling him to her. They kissed deeply, her tongue exploring his mouth, making his dick twitch with interest, even though he had only just cum.

Dave broke her hold and pulled her into a sitting position on the bed.

He held her chin and looked deeply into her eyes. He was pleased when her face cleared and she fell into trance again. He had done a good job here.

'Anthea, can you hear me?' he began.

She nodded, her large eyes never leaving his.

'I have a few more things you need to remember and obey. Is that okay?'

Anthea nodded.

'You will not tell your husband about my visit today, but you will remember it. As far as you are concerned, we have been lovers for a long time, but it's a secret you cannot share.

'If you see me in public, you will pretend you don't know me, but in private you will desire my touch and my love.

'You will obey all my commands willingly.

'You will give yourself to me willingly.

'You will never betray me.

'You will not remember that you have been hypnotised.

'Do you understand?'

Anthea looked steadily at Dave. 'I understand.'

She was so deeply under his control, so completely his, that everything he said became part of her own thoughts and beliefs.

'You are out of trance now,' said Dave.

Anthea's face became more animated, and she stroked Dave's chest.

'Now,' he said. 'I just need the addresses, e-mails and phone numbers of ... who were the other girls again?'

'Charlie, Petra, Nikki and Kym,' replied Anthea. 'I'll get them for you.'

She hopped off the bed and pulled on a dressing gown that was hanging behind the door.

'Come on,' she said. 'I'll make you a cup of tea before you go. Peter won't be back for a long time yet.'

3
Charlie

Dave waded through the letters that had recently dropped through his letterbox. As usual there was nothing there but junk mail and a couple of bill reminders. He would have to get those paid soon.

He thought back to the session with Anthea the other day. That always put him in a good mood. To know that the stuck-up bitch that had lost him the gig at the theatre was now his obedient sex slave – and she clearly loved it. He felt no remorse about this because, deep down, all the women he fucked were totally willing. People didn't realise this, but there was no way you could coerce someone into having sex with you unless they really wanted it. Just like hypnosis could not make one person kill another. So Dave knew that although his hypnotic suggestions worked, it was only because every one of those women secretly wanted to be dominated. They wanted permission to be uninhibited, and Dave gave them that – guilt free – because they just compartmentalised it all. They couldn't help it.

Anthea was a prime example. Dave doubted that her

husband, the Mayor, gave her the kind of attention she craved. It was probably why she and her friends had been so mean-spirited. Deep down they all wanted to hand over control to someone else. Even so, he would still take his revenge, not just with her, but with her friends too, all of whom had been booing him and who had undoubtedly contributed to the situation. He ran through their names again: Charlie, Petra, Nikki and Kym … four women he was going to delight in corrupting and enjoying …

But which one first?

Charlie.

Dave powered up his laptop and started searching for information. He already had Anthea's Facebook details, and was friends with her under an assumed name, so he headed there to see what he could find.

Charlie was there. A pretty, mousy-haired girl with a cute smile. She seemed to be single, as far as he could tell, and she was also trying to quit smoking. Her Facebook page was full of anti-smoking slogans and memes, and yet several pictures of her taken at a variety of clubs and parties showed her with a cigarette in her hand.

This was going to be fairly simple …

Dave picked up his mobile and phoned Anthea. When she answered, he quickly checked that she was alone, and then asked about Charlie.

Dave's conditioning of Anthea meant that he now no longer even needed to use his 'control phrase'; Anthea was conditioned to obey his voice at all times, but to maintain a cool and calm air when anyone else was around. This made it easy for Dave to contact her and use her as he required.

'Hi darling,' said Dave. 'I need some information.'

'Anything, lover,' came the husky response. Anthea

was feeling hot for him again, and would continue to do so ... Just one of the perks.

'Your friend, Charlie? She smokes, right?'

'Charlie Sweeting? Yes, she smokes like a chimney. But she's been trying to stop for ages. Finds she can't get a guy because of it.'

'That's interesting. Do you know if she's tried hypnotherapy?'

'I don't, but I think she probably hasn't.'

'Andrea, I want you to contact Charlie. Make it sound innocent, but say that you've found this great place that is guaranteed to stop her smoking. Tell her that the results are so effective that they offer a money back guarantee that you will never smoke again.'

'Okay.'

'Don't take no for an answer ... and then arrange for her to contact me – or even do it for her – to make an appointment.'

'Yes, I will.' Andrea agreed without hesitation to anything Dave asked. 'Dave ...?'

'Yes, Anthea?'

'When will I see you again? Pete's out of town tonight?'

The thought of spending the evening with Anthea was very appealing indeed.

'I'll come over then,' Dave confirmed. 'Wear something nice for me.'

'I will.'

'Thanks, Anthea. See you later. About 7.00.'

Dave hung up. This was such fun.

At 7.00 on the dot, Dave rang the doorbell at Anthea's house. He was carrying a bottle of wine, and had on a new casual shirt, opened at the collar, and a smart pair of jeans.

The door opened, and Anthea was there.

He knew that he'd asked her to wear something nice, but he wasn't quite prepared for the form-fitting catsuit that she had on. It was mainly black, but patterned with red, orange and yellow flame-like markings that ascended her legs, curved around her hips, and then moved higher to cup her breasts. It was a low-cut halter-neck, which revealed her impressive cleavage. Her hair was teased to perfection, and she had on a pair of silver earrings with ruby stones that matched the colours on her outfit. Her lipstick was also a matching colour, and gleamed as though it had just that moment been applied.

On her feet she wore high-heeled shoes, again with ruby embellishments.

She looked outstanding.

'Well, don't just stand there with your mouth open, come inside!' she said, grinning at the double entendre of her words.

Dave stepped in and watched Anthea's arse as she turned to close the door behind him. It was shapely and sexy as hell, the fabric holding her tightly and giving her ass cheeks something of a lift.

She stalked down the passage toward the living-room. When she reached the door, she gestured to Dave with one finger.

'Come on, then ...'

Dave hurried to catch her up.

The living-room was dark and lit only with candles. Soft music was playing on the radio, or perhaps a CD, and there were cushions all over the floor by the couch.

Anthea curled herself up onto one of the cushions, the

curves of her body moving hypnotically in the flickering light.

Dave took the bottle he had brought and opened it, pouring two glasses of a good, dry red wine and handing one to Anthea.

She took it and thanked him.

They clinked glasses, and Dave sank down onto the cushions beside her. They sat and drank, listening to the music, while Dave stroked his hand on Anthea's leg.

She had her arm around his neck, and was idly stroking the side of it.

Anthea moved closer and started to kiss and nuzzle Dave's neck. He shivered in anticipation, and moved his lips to meet hers.

She sighed and kissed him deeply, her tongue gently playing with his.

After a few moments kissing, she broke off and stood looking down at Dave.

She stepped back and undid the fastening for her halter-neck behind her head.

Dave watched as she let the two strips of material fall, exposing her naked breasts to him.

She smiled seductively and ran her hands over her breasts.

She pulled the cat-suit lower, and peeled it down her legs, revealing no underwear and a freshly shaven pussy.

She looked amazing, and Dave licked his lips.

She pulled off her shoes and let the cat-suit come completely off her body. Then she fell to the floor and with feline grace, moved like some tiger, over to where Dave was sitting.

She kissed him gently on the lips, then started to undo his own shirt. Once that was open, she moved on to his trousers, which were, by now, tenting quite badly from his large hard-on.

He helped her shimmy his trousers and underpants off, and his large cock bobbed in the air before her.

Anthea licked her own lips now, her eyes locked on Dave's. Then she moved her hands to his dick and gently suckled at the end, her tongue teasing the slit there.

Dave shuddered. This was ecstasy.

Anthea regarded Dave's cock, then plunged her mouth down over it, tongue licking around and around. She adjusted her position so that she was braced against one arm, and used the other hand to hold and stroke the shaft.

Dave moaned deep in his throat as his cock disappeared deep into Anthea's. She fellated him with such skill that he thought all his birthdays and Christmases had come at once.

She looked him in the eyes again and, removing his cock from her mouth, said: 'I'm gonna make you cum!'

Then she turned her attention back to his manhood and started sucking on the end, rhythmically stroking her hand around the shaft and gently squeezing his balls when it reached the base.

The rhythm started to get to Dave, and he closed his eyes in pleasure as she slurped and sucked on his cock – as though it was a giant sweet, and she was determined to get the cream from its centre.

She was doing a good job, too. Dave's legs were starting to jerk and tremble as she sucked, and his hands were clenching as the familiar feelings of orgasm started to wash over him.

She was so good at this!

She started to suck and rub him a little faster as she felt his balls clench and his shaft get bigger in preparation for his orgasm.

She didn't stop, and momentarily Dave felt his balls contract and the familiar pumping feeling of cum being driven up his shaft. He cried out, and Anthea moaned as he shot his load into and around her mouth.

She slurped and ate it all up, using her tongue to catch and lick up any stray blobs.

Dave shuddered and came again, the sensations in his cock now intense, and Anthea's sustained licking and sucking continued to send him over the edge.

She gradually slowed her movements, allowing him to soften and recover, but her hand continued to slowly and sensuously stroke his cock, and the ball of her thumb rubbed just below the purple head, on a sensitive spot where Dave just loved being teased.

'My God, Anthea,' said Dave when he could speak. 'That was amazing! Where did you learn to do that?'

Anthea grinned at him. 'It's a special I use on all my lovers.'

She stood and offered him her hand. 'Come on!'

Dave struggled to his feet. 'What?'

'It's my turn!'

Anthea took hold of Dave's cock, which was starting to show interest again, and led him by it out of the living room and up the stairs to the bedroom.

Dave sighed … You really couldn't get too much of a good thing!

Once in her bedroom, Anthea lay back on the bed and opened her legs.

'Time to reciprocate,' she said.

Dave crawled up between her legs and looked down at her beautiful pussy lips: they were small and neat. He opened her up with his fingers and bent his head. He ran his tongue gently over her clitoris. Anthea squirmed.

Yes, she was such a good subject. And, Dave realised, it was a stroke of genius making her believe they were regular lovers. It meant that Anthea's own imagination and desires made her react and behave just like she would if this had been the case to begin with.

Anthea rolled her hips into Dave's face. A few minutes later she was screaming her orgasm into the room.

Two hours later, Dave left Anthea's house. He was chilled and happy, and whistled a tune, slightly off key, as he returned to his car.

He had fucked Anthea twice more in the bedroom; first from behind, causing her to scream and thrash and cum all over his dick several times, and then slow and hard in the missionary position, her legs as wide as they could go to allow him maximum penetration.

He had left her lying on the bed in a little puddle of post-orgasmic pleasure, smiling and drifting.

As he had dressed, he had arranged for Anthea to contact Charlie about her smoking problem, and to insist that she come accompany her to see Dave at his flat. She wasn't to allow Charlie any choice in the matter ... and Anthea could be quite persuasive.

Anthea had agreed to make sure they were both there the next afternoon, at 3.00 on the dot, and then had blown Dave a kiss as he left the house.

On his drive home, Dave planned out how and what he was going to do with Charlie.

Anthea had been a revelation. A perfect hypnotic subject, and an amazing lover, and he wondered how Charlie would fare.

Charlie seemed to have more than just a smoking

problem. All the pictures of her on her Facebook showed her wearing baggy, shapeless, colourless clothes. It was as though she was ashamed of her body. Her hair was often a wild mess too, and she wore little or no make-up. No wonder she didn't have a boyfriend.

He had also done a little checking into the other three girls, Petra, Nikki and Kym. He knew that they were all single, but that Nikki and Kym both had boyfriends. Nikki was black, and her boyfriend was one of the local college's basketball team. He was not only handsome and fit, but was also was rumoured to have an enormous dick – at least, judging from the light-hearted Facebook messages that Dave had seen.

So maybe giving one of the other girls a little taste of that would be interesting …

Dave parked up and headed to his flat. He had some tidying to do before tomorrow's session.

At 3.00 pm exactly the following day, the buzzer rang at Dave's door. He was ready for his visitors.

He opened the door to find Anthea and Charlie standing there. Anthea smiled to see him, but Charlie looked suspicious.

'Hello ladies,' said Dave. 'Good to see you, and thanks for coming.'

He ushered them into his flat, and through into the kitchen area, where he had a couple of cups of tea ready. Anthea accepted hers, but Charlie declined. She was not going to be easy.

Anthea was wearing a smart pants suit, and her make-up and hair were, as usual, impeccable. But Charlie was wearing a pair of scruffy jeans, a sloppy, shapeless T-shirt and a hoodie jacket. Her brown hair was scraped back in a ponytail and held with a cheap scrunchie.

'So, Charlie is it? Anthea tells me that you want to stop smoking?'

Charlie shot a look at Anthea. 'Yes I do.'

'That's good,' said Dave. 'May I ask why?'

Charlie's eyes narrowed. 'Why do you need to know that?'

'It's simply that, as I work with you, it's helpful to me to understand what your motivations are. It helps me to guide you to removing the compulsion.'

Charlie nodded; it seemed to make sense to her. 'Well ... I've not had a boyfriend in over a year now, and all the men I meet are put off by the smoking,' she explained. Dave nodded sympathetically as she continued. 'All's fine at first, but then they lose interest and drift away. The last one said that I stank.'

'Oh, you don't stink,' said Anthea.

'I bloody do!' retorted Charlie. 'When I pick my clothes up the morning after I've been out, I can smell the smoke on them. It's horrible.'

'... And yet you still smoke,' said Dave.

Charlie nodded. 'I just can't seem to break the habit. It's a vicious circle. I smoke when I get lonely and down, and I get lonely and down because I smoke ... so ...'

'Well, I'm sure I can help you,' said Dave.

'Would you mind waiting here, Anthea?' asked Dave. 'And Charlie, would you come with me?'

Dave stood and gestured to the door. 'We're just going into the living-room. It's more comfortable there, and easier to discuss this with you.'

'Okay. But Anthea will be here the whole time?'

'Yes I will,' said Anthea. 'Now go!'

Charlie allowed herself to be ushered into the other room.

Dave had prepared it with some dim lighting, and a special relaxation CD ready to play on the stereo.

He gestured to the armchair, which was covered with throws and looked very comfortable. 'Can you sit there, Charlie?'

Charlie sat, but she was on edge. 'I'm glad that Anthea's here too,' she said.

'Let me just check she's all right too,' said Dave. 'I'll be right back.'

Dave left the room and returned to the kitchen, where Anthea was sitting waiting. She smiled at Dave when he entered.

'She's going to be all right, isn't she?' Anthea asked.

'She's going to be fine,' said Dave.

He reached out his hand and touched Anthea on the shoulder. 'Trance Anthea.'

Her body and face relaxed, and she sat forward a little, eager to hear anything that Dave might say or command of her.

'Just wait here, Anthea,' said Dave. 'I won't be long, but when Charlie comes out, she may be a little … different … You're not to make any adverse comment, but to support her. Do you understand?'

'I understand,' said Anthea.

'So for now, Anthea, just wait.'

Dave left Anthea sitting with her eyes closed, deep in trance. She would hear and see nothing of what happened.

Back in the other room, Dave found Charlie still sitting.

'Everything okay?' she asked.

'Fine,' said Dave. 'Are you comfortable?'

'Yes,' said Charlie a little defensively.

'Okay. Let's start. Charlie, I want you to close your eyes and listen to the sounds …'

Dave reached across and flicked on the CD player. The gentle sounds of an ocean filtered through the speakers. Waves on a shale beach, gently rushing in and out.

Charlie closed her eyes and settled into the armchair. She clasped her arms together over her stomach and crossed her feet.

'That's good,' said Dave gently. 'Just listen to the sound of the waves. In and out. In and out.'

'Now, Charlie. Hypnotism just feels like being relaxed. Completely relaxed. Like just before you fall asleep at night, when your body relaxes and your mind starts to drift.

'All you have to do is relax, listen to my voice and the sounds from the CD, and agree with the suggestions I put to you. Do you think you can do that, Charlie?'

'Yes,' nodded Charlie.

Dave could tell by her breathing that she was already relaxing into a state where he could work her.

'Charlie, I want you to take a deep breath in now for five seconds. One. Two. Three. Four. Five. That's excellent. Now hold ... and exhale for three seconds. One. Two. Three.

'And again, Charlie. In ... Two. Three. Four. Five. Hold ... and out. Two. Three.

'Now Charlie, imagine you're standing on the shore, watching the waves wash in and out. There's a staircase in front of you leading down. It's easy to step onto it, and now we'll count the steps as you descend.

'One. Two. Three ...'

As Dave spoke, so Charlie felt herself relaxing deeper. In her mind she could see the beautiful azure sea and hear the waves washing. She could see the staircase, and as she descended, so she felt waves of relaxation wash over her.

Dave could see that she was drifting under. Her

hands were not held together so tightly now, and she had slumped even further into the sofa.

'Can you hear me, Charlie?'

'Mmmph ss,' she mumbled.

'There's a door at the bottom of the steps. What colour is it?'

''ss gree.'

'Excellent. You're doing very well. Very good, Charlie. So open that green door and step through.

'Can you see what's beyond?'

'Yss.'

'Describe it to me.'

'Sss a meadow. Trees. Quiet.'

'Very good, Charlie. You are doing so, so well. So go into the meadow now. Feel the warm grass under your feet. Smell the scent of the trees.'

Charlie smiled as, in her mind, she did as instructed. The meadow felt good.

'You see, Charlie? Doing as I say makes you feel good, doesn't it?'

'Yss.'

'You like feeling this good Charlie, don't you?'

'Yss.'

'Very good. Now, you wanted me to help you with something didn't you?'

'Yss.'

'What was it Charlie?'

''moking.'

'Excellent. Every time you make me happy Charlie, you feel happy yourself. It makes you feel good to make me happy, doesn't it Charlie?'

'Yss.'

'You like feeling good, don't you?'

'Yss.'

'You like making me happy, don't you?'
'Yss.'
'So, smoking. This doesn't make me happy. And it doesn't make you feel good, does it?'

Charlie's face creased slightly, understanding the inescapable logic of what Dave was saying. Eventually, almost imperceptibly, she shook her head.

'I can't hear you, Charlie. Hearing you makes me happy. Can you tell me?'

Her face cleared and she said, 'No.'

'That's good, Charlie. Excellent. So smoking is not for you. It doesn't make you happy, and it doesn't make me happy. You need to stop.

'Smoking doesn't make you happy, Charlie. So the desire to do it is now going away. And as it goes away, so you make me happy. What happens when you make me happy, Charlie?'

'Makes me happy.'

'That's really good, Charlie. I am so very happy with you right now.'

Charlie smiled in her trance. It was good to make Dave happy. Doing so made her happy. And that was good.

'So, now that you won't smoke anymore, we need to find other ways for you to make me happy. Would you like that, Charlie? Do you want to make me happy?'

'Yes.'

Dave smiled. He had her.

'Listen to me carefully, Charlie. There are some things I need to tell you.'

About an hour later, Dave left the living-room and returned to the kitchen. Anthea was still sitting there, eyes closed, exactly as he had left her.

'Wake up, Anthea,' said Dave. And Anthea reacted as though she had just been switched on. She raised her head, opened her eyes and smiled at Dave.

'Oh, hi Dave,' she said. 'Is Charlie done now?'

'Oh yes,' said Dave with a smile. 'She's completely ready.

'Charlie? Would you come through please?'

Charlie appeared at the doorway, eyes gleaming. 'Oh. My. God. Anthea. That was so amazing. Dave has completely cured me. I mean, I have just no desire whatsoever for a cigarette. In fact …'

She rummaged in her bag, which was sitting by the kitchen table, and removed a pack of twenty, from which just two cigarettes had been used.

'… This is what I think of these.'

She opened the kitchen bin and threw the cigarettes in.

'Urgh, horrible things. Never want to smoke them again!'

'That's brilliant,' said Anthea.

'I know! Isn't it.' Charlie was full of enthusiasm. 'I've just got some more things to go over with Dave. It's gonna take another half hour or so, so you can get off if you want.'

'Oh, okay. That's good, as I have some errands to run.'

'Okay then. I'll call you later.' Charlie hugged Anthea. 'Thanks again for bringing me here. He's the best …'

She smiled at Dave as she said it, and Dave felt that familiar tugging in his groin.

'It's my pleasure,' he said. 'Let me show you out, Anthea.'

He escorted Anthea to the door and opened it for her.

'Hope it won't be too long before I see you again.'

She wrinkled her nose and winked at him. 'Me too, lover,' she said, and kissed him gently on the mouth.

With that, she was off and away.

Dave turned back to Charlie, who was exploring the cupboards in the kitchen.

'I'm thirsty,' she said. 'Is that a side-effect?'

'Yes,' said Dave. 'It can be. Let me get you a glass of something. Red or white?'

'Oh, that's kind,' Charlie enthused. 'Red please.'

Dave poured them both a glass of Merlot and returned to the living room. Charlie sat back on the sofa, her knees together, sipping her wine and looking at Dave over the rim.

'So, where did you discover you could do this?' she asked.

'Do this?' asked Dave.

'Help people stop smoking,' she clarified.

'Oh, it's just a knack,' he said. 'Put your glass down, Charlie.'

Charlie obeyed.

'Now Charlie. Sex time.'

Charlie's eyes fluttered briefly as her brain fell into trance and processed the subliminal command, and then she looked at Dave. Her mouth split in an enormous grin, and she squealed with delight. 'Oh, I thought you'd never ask! How do you want me?'

Dave thought for a second, then said, 'Naked. Now.'

Charlie grinned and started pulling off her clothes.

Dave had been disappointed with how she had dressed. It was as though she was embarrassed to be female somehow. As she undressed, he could see that, like Anthea, she had a good body. There was shape in her waist and her boobs were small.

Soon she was standing in front of Dave wearing nothing at all. Her shape was a little boyish, if Dave was honest, but she was slim and attractive. There was an unruly mass of brown hair over her pubis – she obviously didn't shave – and she seemed pretty comfortable with being naked. But, then again, that was what he had told her to be …

Dave led her to his bedroom, and there he gazed deep into her eyes once more, sending her into a deep trance.

'Charlie. Can you hear me?'

Charlie stood with her eyes closed. 'Yes,' she said slowly.

'Open your eyes.'

Charlie opened her eyes, but she stared straight ahead. There was no life in her at all. Dave smiled to himself. She had been so easy to control after all. He wondered if he should make some other changes to her … after all, she seemed to be having little luck with men the way she was.

'Charlie,' he said, 'today you are a fuck-toy. My fuck-toy. You exist only to fuck my brains out, and you will do everything you can to please me. Do you understand?'

Charlie blinked. 'Yes.'

'So what are you?'

'I am a fuck-toy. Your fuck-toy.'

'So what are you waiting for?'

Charlie shook her head as though she was waking, but remained deep in the trance that Dave had put her in. She looked at him, and he saw the changes taking place across her pretty face as her gaze travelled to his cock, which was standing to attention.

She looked at him with desire and lust, and her eyes narrowed slightly as she reached for him.

Next thing Dave knew, he was on his back, on the bed, and Charlie was between his legs, sucking and stroking his cock as though it was the tastiest delight that she had ever sampled.

Dave moaned as she caressed his balls with one hand, while stroking his shaft with the other and gently suckling at the tip with her mouth. Her tongue lashed out greedily and curled around him, and her cheeks sucked in each time she engulfed him in her mouth.

It was ecstasy!

Dave let her suck him for ten minutes or so, savouring the sensations of her lips, tongue and hands on his dick. Then he told her to stop, and instead asked her to position herself to receive him from behind. She obeyed instantly, lifting her little bum to him and looking back at him.

'Fuck me now,' she growled.

Dave grinned. He was always happy to oblige a willing client.

Dave stroked his cock with his hand. He was fully erect and it felt brilliant. He could feel his own stiffness, and his dick stood out from his body proudly.

He knelt behind Charlie and positioned the head of his cock at the entrance to her vagina. She wriggled her ass sexily, impatient for him.

Placing his hands on her hips, he gently manoeuvred his cock into her pussy, letting it slide in. She was soaking wet, ready for him, and he felt the sides of her cunt expand to allow him entry.

When he was buried deep inside her, he paused for a moment, savouring the feeling of his dick being gripped from all sides, then he drew it slowly out again. He started to fuck Charlie slowly, holding her hips and letting his dick do the work.

Charlie started to moan. He could feel the walls of her sensitive pussy start to ripple and clench on him as he moved. So he moved faster.

Charlie moaned some more, and wiggled her ass again. Dave took this as a sign that he was on the right track, and so fucked her faster.

He set up a rhythm with her. As she bucked back against his dick, so he slammed it into her, his balls tapping against her sensitive clit on each inward stroke.

She started to breath heavily, in time with his fucking, and so moderated the motion so that it was in time with her gasps, which were coming harder and faster now.

'Oh ... oh ... oh ... yes ... oh ...' she moaned in time with his strokes.

Her voice grew louder as she drew closer and closer to the point of no return.

'Oh ... oh ... God ... yes ... yes ... yesyesyesI'mcumming!'

She collapsed onto the bed, hands clenching the duvet as an orgasm rippled through her. She lost all sense of rhythm, but Dave continued to fuck her through the intense pleasure that she was feeling.

She thrashed her head back and forth, babbling incoherently. Then she screamed again as another orgasm took her.

She was cumming continuously onto his dick, Dave realised, pausing a moment to withdraw it from her pussy, and seeing that it was completely coated with her juices. He pushed it back in and continued to fuck Charlie some more. She quietened a little at first, but then crested again, crying out in pleasure as a third, harder orgasm took her body, making her shake and spasm on her hands and knees in front of Dave.

He withdrew and stroked her ass with his hands,

kneading her waist and hips as she came down from the plateau he had taken her to.

She collapsed forward onto her elbows and wiped the hair from her eyes.

'My God, Dave,' she said, looking back at him. 'I've never cum that hard before. Never.'

She laughed to herself and sprawled on the bed. Then she scooted around and pushed Dave back.

'Now it's your turn,' she announced, and locked her lips around the swollen head of his dick.

Already quite sensitive from fucking her pussy, Dave felt triggers of electricity spread through his body. Charlie grasped his dick with her hand and wanked him gently, teasing the head with her lips.

She looked him in the eyes and smiled. 'I'm gonna make you cum, mister,' she said with a mischievous grin.

Then she sank her mouth down over his dick and started to suck him in earnest, one hand teasing and stroking his balls and perineum, while the other squeezed his shaft.

After a few minutes of this, Dave felt his own orgasm approaching. Charlie continued to work him, providing the rhythm he needed, and Dave's legs started to shake as his orgasm approached.

He felt the cum start to settle in his balls, which tightened, and his dick swelled slightly.

Then he was cumming! He could feel the familiar pumping sensation as the cum shot up his dick, and he watched as Charlie expertly sucked it from him as though she was drinking a milkshake. She sucked and licked, emphasising the sensations for Dave, who fell back against the bed, moaning and squirming as his balls were sucked dry by Charlie's talented mouth.

When he had stopped pumping cum into her mouth,

she sucked him a little longer, then grinned at him. She opened her mouth to show him that it was empty. She had swallowed all his essence down. Then she licked him clean of any remaining cum – his and hers, as his dick had been liberally coated with her juices too – and released him from her mouth with a pop.

'How was that?' she asked, eager to know that she had done a good job. Dave realised that this was part of the programming he had instilled in her. She was a fuck-toy and wanted ... no, needed ... to please him.

'That was amazing, Charlie,' said Dave, and she beamed at him. Happy that she had done a good job.

Dave lay back and looked at his most recent subject. She was good-looking, there was no doubt about that, but there were certainly some things that he would change about her.

'Charlie,' he said. 'You're back to normal now. You're not a fuck-toy any longer. You're normal Charlie, but still completely under my command. Do you understand?'

Charlie's eyes flickered, a blankness crossing them as Dave's instruction took hold. 'I understand.'

'Excellent. Now, Charlie, take me back to your house ... to where you live.'

Charlie nodded, smiling at Dave.

The two of them got dressed and headed out. Charlie had a car, and so drove Dave back to her flat, which was about ten minutes away.

Once there, Dave asked her to show him the clothes that she liked to wear.

Dave sat on her bed as Charlie pulled out several long-sleeved blouses and over-the-knee skirts. It was all fairly basic stuff; very sensible 'librarian' type outfits. Nothing that would arouse or titillate any man ... unless they were specifically into that sort of 'old maid' look on a young girl.

'What do you do for a job, Charlie,' asked Dave.

'I work as a receptionist,' she replied. 'At the bank.'

That explained a lot, thought Dave. Well he had no wish to get her fired. And the thought surprised him, especially since she and her friends had caused him to lose his own job.

'We're going to make a few changes, Charlie,' said Dave. 'Come here.'

Charlie came and sat by Dave on the bed.

Dave reached up his hand and stroked her cheek.

'Sleep Charlie,' he said, gazing deep into her eyes, and instantly she obeyed, drifting off into a dreamless sleep, where all she could hear was the sound of his voice as he told her what clothes she should prefer to wear from now on ... He suggested some other things too ... things that she would find arousing and that might help her get a boyfriend.

Charlie drifted and relaxed. Everything that Dave said was good ... she would do everything he said ... he made her so happy ...

4
Petra

Dave checked his notes on Petra. Anthea had done a good job in providing him with details of the girls, but it always helped to do his own research, just in case.

Petra was an interesting one. She had had a long-term boyfriend in the past, but it had all ended messily, and so, for the time being, she was happy to be single.

But she certainly liked men, and this was where the boyfriends of Nikki and Kym came in. Dave realised that he would need to involve them if he was to get full enjoyment of the delights of all these women, and breaking Petra would seem to be the way to do it.

Anthea had told him that Petra was probably the most strong-willed of all the girls, and so he thought that a little demonstration would help to break her down so that he could get inside her ... mentally and physically.

First of all, though, Dave had to get to the boyfriends of the other girls. A quick hour of Facebook stalking later, and Dave knew that Nikki's boyfriend was called Tyrone, and that he was going to the nearby university, studying Media of all things ... but he was also in the basketball team, on account of his height – he was just shy of seven feet tall, and yet he was only twenty years old. Nikki had bagged herself a toyboy!

Dave thought on this for a few moments, then picked up his phone and dialled the university. A few minutes later, he had been put through to the sports coach there, and was offering to run a complimentary session for the basketball team on relaxation and effective self-motivation. The coach was intrigued, and so Dave arranged an appointment for the following week to go to see him and discuss it further. This also gave Dave time to create some impressive-looking certificates of his qualifications in the field – not all made-up, as Dave had indeed studied psychology and various relaxation techniques. So he knew what he was talking about.

As it was a Friday afternoon, Dave decided that he wanted a bit of a night out, and so considered who he should call up. Anthea was simply delightful, but he had been seeing – and servicing – her regularly for some weeks now. Sally was still available too, of course … But he really fancied seeing how Charlie was turning out. It had been around a week since his first session with her, and he was intrigued to see how she had interpreted and carried out his instructions.

He opened his phone and found her number. One thing he had discovered, since he started his little habit of mesmerising women, was that if they had one of the more modern smart-phones, then he could programme it to play a specific tune when he called them. The latest models could play a different ringtone for every caller, if you wanted, and this feature allowed Dave to set up one specific to his number and then implant in the girls a post-hypnotic command to slip into trance whenever they heard it. He could have put them under via the call itself, but he liked the idea that by the time he spoke to them, they were already completely attuned to his words.

He selected Charlie's number and waited while it rang. After a moment, Charlie answered.

'Hello?'

'Hi Charlie, it's Dave.'

'Hi Dave. How's it going?'

'Are you alone, Charlie?'

'I am.'

'Excellent. Have you any plans for tonight, Charlie?'

'No.'

'You have now. Meet me at 8.00 pm at Bar Rouge on the High Street.'

'Yes.'

Charlie's voice had a slightly robotic note to it, and Dave could tell that she was deep in trance.

'Who am I, Charlie?' he asked.

'My master,' Charlie replied without hesitation.

Excellent.

'So, meet me tonight, Charlie. And wear something nice. You're just meeting with me as your therapist, to check that everything's all right. Do you understand?'

'I do.'

Dave cut the call, and smiled. So he was now set for the evening. He wondered what Charlie might interpret as 'something nice'. He guessed he would find out very soon.

Dave was sitting at the bar in Bar Rouge. He had arrived there just before 8.00, and had checked that his reservation for a table for two was in place. Then he had settled down to wait with a gin and tonic for Charlie to arrive.

As he sat and sipped his drink, he looked around at all the others in the bar. Couples, for the most part, but a few singletons sitting, like he was, either waiting for their friends or hoping to make new ones. It was the same all over.

There was a slight commotion over by the door, and Dave looked across.

Charlie was there. But unless he had known it was her, he would never have recognised her.

Gone was the shy, mousy little girl, and in her place ...

For a start, her hair was no longer a mousy brown. She had clearly visited a hairdresser who really knew what they were doing, and now one side of her head was shaven to a thick stubble, while the rest of her hair was styled into a choppy drift of brown and blonde that cascaded around her head into a longer, layered bob on the other side.

Her face was made-up with pristine foundation, colour and subtle kohl emphasising her eyes, which glowed with confidence, and her lips were a bright, glossy red.

Dave's astonished eyes drifted down the rest of her body.

She was wearing a loose silk blouse, cut to accentuate her slim figure. It clung to her breasts and revealed a deep cleavage that she had previously kept hidden on all occasions.

On her legs she had a pair of stylish brown leatherette trousers, slim-legged, which hugged the curves of her waist and bottom. On her feet she wore a simple pair of shiny high-heeled shoes, brown to match her trousers.

Dave realised that he was gawping and made a concerted effort to close his mouth.

Charlie scanned the crowd in the bar, saw Dave and

waved to him. She said something to the bouncer on the door – it seemed that he had been trying to get her number or something – and walked across the floor to him, her legs and ass swaying with a motion that got just about every male pair of eyes in the place on her.

'Hi, Dave,' she said as she approached. 'Sorry I'm a little late. Cab driver refused to let me out unless I gave him my number.'

'I hope you didn't give it to him,' said Dave. He really had no idea what to say!

'Of course not!' Charlie giggled. 'I gave him a fake one. Doesn't everyone do that?' She sank onto the bar stool beside him. 'I've never been in here before,' she said, looking around with interest.

'Really?' said Dave. 'It's supposed to be very nice.'

Charlie nodded. 'So, get me a drink then!'

Dave grinned. 'What would you like?'

'Vodka Coke please.'

Dave ordered up the drink, and watched Charlie as she looked around the bar, smiling and excited to be there.

This was such an incredible change in her, and Dave congratulated himself. Not only had he stopped her smoking, but he seemed to have given her a whole new lease of life too.

The drink arrived, and they clinked and drank. Charlie seemed happy to be there, relaxed and casual, and lots of fun too. She was chatty, and their conversation ranged from the latest films, to pop videos to food programmes that they liked to watch on television. She was a fan of Gordon Ramsey and liked seeing him ball people out, and she also loved watching the *Come Dine With Me* shows where four strangers cooked each other meals and then gave them marks out of ten.

Over dinner, Dave watched Charlie critically. She was a completely different girl from the one who had been at his flat a week ago. This Charlie was happy and chatty and flirty ... everything that the other Charlie had not been.

'Charlie,' he said, during a break in the conversation. 'You seem very different from when we met last week. Can I ask, have you had any urge to smoke since our session?'

Charlie shook her head. 'No, not at all. You seem to have completely cured me of that filthy habit.'

'And what about the rest?' said Dave. 'You seem a lot ... happier?'

Charlie grinned. 'Well, since I saw you, Dave, I've been thinking about my life, my choices, my habits and whatever, and realised that if I wanted to enjoy myself, I had to start looking like I did ...'

Dave smiled. This was indeed what he had programmed her to think.

Charlie continued. 'And anyway, what's the point of hiding under a sack your whole life? You want to make the most of it!'

She picked up her glass and downed the remains of her drink.

A waiter came and took the empty plates away. Dave had to admit that Charlie was good company. He had also noticed every man in the bar looking at her at one point or another. She was not going to be going home alone that night.

As he looked at her, he again let his eyes drift over her amazing transformation. Her hair was incredible, and her personality shone. His eyes rested on her cleavage for a moment, and as she shifted, he saw under her blouse, small raised areas around her left nipple.

It seemed that one of his other instructions had been carried out too, and she had got a piercing. He smiled. It was good to know that he had the control when he wanted it.

The waiter returned to the table – and, Dave noticed, couldn't keep his eyes off Charlie either, as he asked if they had finished and wanted the bill.

Charlie smiled at Dave and suggested to him that they split it. Dave was happy with this, and so they settled up.

As they stood, there was a slight murmuring at the bar, and Charlie looked across to where a group of men were standing watching.

She grinned at Dave. 'If you're off home, I think I'll stay for another drink.'

Dave smiled. 'Sure, no problem.'

They hugged briefly, and Dave took his leave as Charlie headed to the bar and the gaggle of men there. Her ass looked amazing in the leather jeans, Dave thought; and as she got to the bar, three of the men immediately started talking to her, and one gestured to the barman for drinks.

She was going to be all right.

Dave headed out and back to his flat. He had to prepare for his meeting the following week, and the next stages in his plan to get Petra.

As Dave had expected, his meeting with the university sports coach had gone well. Not really surprising, as he had read up in advance on various NLP techniques for interviewing, and on the background to the university. That sound preparation, along with his ability to read body language, and a little hypnotic suggestion along the way, had ensured that it all went smoothly.

So it was that, a week later, Dave was running the first of his sessions with the basketball team. These were supposed to be team-building and motivational sessions, and indeed, that was what Dave would be doing ... in part ... but his main focus was to get inside the mind of Tyrone ...

'I want all of you to close your eyes and try to relax,' said Dave.

Around him, lying on the floor of the university gym, were ten of the basketball players. Each of them just 20 or 21 years old, but all of them over six feet tall! There was a fair mix of races and skin colours too, from a Chinese guy to a couple of Indian chaps, and of course Tyrone, who was a black Nigerian. There were white guys there too. All of them were lying on gym mats, trying to relax as part of the session that Dave had set up.

Dave walked among them, keeping his eye on them all. Sometimes group hypnosis worked on everyone, but it wasn't often. Usually, one or two people would go under, a smattering more would fall into just a light sleep, but the majority would simply think it a bit silly and play along for laughs. Like all good stage hypnotists, Dave had become pretty adept at telling the difference.

'I want you to keep your eyes closed, and in your mind count backwards from one hundred. With each number, you'll drift further into relaxation.'

Dave watched as the assembled young men started to try to follow his instructions.

He moved closer to Tyrone, and looked intently at

him. He had his eyes closed, and his lips were moving slightly as he counted down.

'That's good, Tyrone,' said Dave gently by his ear. 'Very good. Just keep counting down. Further and further down. Very good. And listen to my voice.'

Dave kept his own voice quiet so that only Tyrone could hear him.

'You're doing very well, Tyrone. Very good. Deeper and deeper. Relax with the sound of my voice. Deeper. Keep counting, getting slower now. Slowly. Counting. And as you count, you find yourself slipping into a deep, deep sleep. Oh, you are so tired. Deep, deep sleep, listening to my voice.'

Dave noted that Tyrone's breathing was steadying. The boy was indeed falling into a deep sleep.

'Very, very good Tyrone. Very good. Now sleep on my command, Tyrone. Sleep. And as you fall into this deep sleep, you'll obey my commands. It feels good to obey. To be part of the team, to follow instructions. It feels good, and makes you happy to be in my team, to follow my instructions. Deeper and deeper ...'

Dave's crooning voice penetrated Tyrone's head, and finally the boy succumbed to his instructions, falling into a deep hypnotic trance. Dave saw that his face relaxed, his lips slowed and stopped moving, and his hands lay loosely on his chest.

Dave stood up and checked on the rest of the lads. They were all still lying there. One at the back was smiling and trying to suppress some giggles. This was normal.

Dave took them through a series of motivational situations, emphasising teamwork and success. If even a little of this penetrated their thick skulls, then it would have been worthwhile.

All the time, Tyrone lay motionless and silent, deep in

the trance that Dave had induced in him.

Every so often, Dave would crouch by the young man and give him more suggestions, implanting certain behaviours in him, and linking them to success and to the pleasure of obeying Dave. It was a tried and trusted technique – at least in Dave's book.

Eventually, the hour was up, and so Dave started the process of bringing the boys up out of their trances. Some just stretched and yawned. For them, it had been a bit of a lark to lie there for an hour or so; far better than an hour of strenuous gym work. Others lay there for a bit, coming out of the sleep they had been in.

For Tyrone, it was as if he had drifted off somewhere. He had the memory of something really nice having happened to him, and of having loved being there ... but not much else.

The lads all got up, stood around looking a bit embarrassed, and then headed off to the changing room to get back into their regular clothes.

Dave called Tyrone back, asking him to wait a moment.

'Everything okay?' asked Tyrone.

'Sure,' said Dave. 'I just wanted to check in with you. How did the session go for you?'

'Can't say I know,' said Tyrone. He ran his hand over his head. 'Slept through most of it.'

Dave smiled. 'That can happen.'

'That all, boss?' asked Tyrone.

Dave clocked that everyone else had now left.

'Just one more thing, Tyrone. Happy place.'

Tyrone looked puzzled for a second, but then his face cleared and relaxed, and he stood there looking into space.

Dave grinned to himself. Excellent.

'Tyrone,' he said. 'Take off your shorts.'

Without any hesitation, the big man started to pull down his shorts.

Dave stopped him. 'Stop. That's okay. You don't have to take your shorts off. Tyrone, whenever I say "happy place", you will return to this state, and you will obey my commands. Do you understand?'

'I understand.'

'Excellent. Now, back to normal Tyrone, and go and get yourself dressed.'

Tyrone blinked and grinned. 'Sure boss,' he said, and loped off to join the others.

Dave had to resist rubbing his hands together, but he was delighted. Now he had another hypnotic subject to add to his growing band ... and now he could start to get back at Petra.

Petra Smith. Petra hated her name. It was boring as hell. Just like her life!

Just like every morning she left her flat and made her way to the bus stop.

Just like every morning she got the bus to work.

Just like every day she worked all day, with no break for lunch.

Just like every day she got the bus home again.

No wonder she looked forward to the evenings!

What she really loved was getting together with her girlfriends and making some hell somewhere. She never minded where ... just somewhere she could sit and drink and generally rip the shit out of anyone who got in her way!

Maybe this was why she was still single. All her friends had found men they could go away with, or marry, or live with, or fuck the shit out of ... and sometimes all of the above. Even Charlie, the mouse of the group, had suddenly improved herself and had men falling all over her. But Petra was unlucky in love.

She wasn't unattractive, either. She had blonde hair that cascaded down her back. She was carrying a little weight around her stomach and hips, the result of too many vodka shots and bottles of wine, but her breasts were nice and perky, and she thought she had good legs too.

All these thoughts pressed against Petra's brain as she made her way back home after work. As usual, she was also worrying about what to eat, whether or not there was anything in the fridge, or whether or not it would be last weekend's leftover curry. Again.

She grimaced. The curry had been nice enough, but then, after having it three days in a row, the pleasure had started to fade.

She turned the corner to her street, and walked headlong into someone who was standing on the path.

Her bag went flying, and a pile of papers that the man had been carrying also flew everywhere.

'Oh, I'm sorry. I'm so sorry!' she blurted, and started picking up the papers.

The man started doing the same, and also collecting the contents of her bag, stuffing the various items back in.

It wasn't until he stood, and she got a good look at him, that she recognised him.

'Tyrone?'

It was Nikki's boyfriend. Petra had met him a couple of times at social occasions, but hadn't really clocked him. He was with Nikki, after all, and that made him a no-go zone for her.

Tyrone looked down at her and grinned. 'It's Petra,

isn't it? Oh, man, I'm so sorry. Just wasn't looking where I was going.'

'What are you doing here, anyway?' asked Petra. 'Isn't Nikki's place across town?'

Tyrone looked sad. 'Sure is, but me and Nikki, we've not been getting on too well of late.'

Petra saw Tyrone's face fall, and felt sorry for him. 'Oh, I'm sorry to hear that, Tyrone.'

'Yeah,' he said, picking up the last of Petra's things and handing her the bag.

Petra had a handful of papers, and shuffled them into a neater pile before handing them to Tyrone.

'So, what are you up to?' she asked.

'Well. Nuthin.'

Petra looked at Tyrone. He was tall, but lean and athletic. No wonder he was the star of the basketball team. His hands were very big as well, and she had to stifle a wicked grin and she wondered if this was an indication of something large elsewhere.

Petra was what her girlfriends often termed 'a one'. She enjoyed one-night stands on occasion. She would chat up random strangers she met on their nights out, and then take them home for a night of debauchery, dumping them the next day. Her friends had got used to her lurid descriptions of what she got up to with her conquests, and secretly enjoyed hearing her tales of shagging with no strings attached.

But they all had a rule. Husbands and boyfriends were off limits. They could do whatever they wanted, but hands off each other's men ...

But if Tyrone was having problems with Nikki, well, that wasn't Petra's fault, was it? And maybe he needed someone to talk to ...

'Do you fancy a drink?' asked Petra before she could

have second thoughts. 'You look like you could do with one.'

Tyrone smiled again. 'Sure. I ain't got nuthin else going on.'

He stuffed the papers he was carrying into a bag over his shoulder, and he and Petra headed across the street, making for a nearby wine bar.

From his car, parked a little way down the road, Dave watched them go. He was pleased that Petra hadn't thought to question Tyrone more about why he was there, or to pay closer attention to the sheets of paper he was carrying, which had conveniently gone everywhere when she had walked into him.

Tyrone, for his part, had proved an excellent subject, taking the suggestion that his relationship with Nikki was rocky, and picking up the idea that he was attracted to Petra.

Dave was very good at making his subjects totally believe what he told them, and Tyrone was about to give Petra the fucking of her life, though she didn't know it yet.

Dave started his car and headed off back to his own flat. He had a few hours before he would return ... as soon as Tyrone had done what he had been instructed to do.

Petra laughed loudly as Tyrone told her another joke, about a policeman and a parrot. He was great company, and as the wine had flowed, so she had heard a little about his problems with Nikki. Not that she was particularly bothered.

Every time she looked at Tyrone, she saw a handsome man with a lovely smile. The wine had also done what it usually did, and made her horny as fuck. She couldn't keep her eyes off the front of his trousers, and as the evening progressed, she took every opportunity she could to rub up to him and press herself on and against him.

Tyrone was also having a good time. Somewhere in the back of his mind something nagged that he had known this would happen, but he wasn't bothered. Petra was good company and not unattractive to the eye. He liked the way his black skin looked against her pale body, and enjoyed touching her arm as they chatted. The wine had flowed, and he was feeling very mellow indeed.

Petra picked up her glass and downed the remaining wine. 'That's it. I'm done!' she announced with a satisfied grin.

Tyrone smiled back and downed his glass too. The bottle was indeed empty.

'D'ya fancy a coffee?' asked Petra.

'Sure,' said Tyrone, and he made to go to the bar.

Petra reached out her hand and stopped him. 'At my place,' she said. 'Come on.'

She grabbed her bag, and all but hauled Tyrone out of the seat. She marvelled again at how tall he was. She was only 5 feet 6 inches, and Tyrone, at close to 7 feet tall, towered over her.

She took his hand, enjoying the feel of it in hers, and also liking the contrast of black and white skins. Together they made their way out the bar and into the street.

Petra laughed, and tugged Tyrone back to her flat, which was only a couple of streets away.

When they arrived, she fumbled in her bag for her keys and finally got the door open. She tumbled in, Tyrone behind her, and as he closed the door, she held onto him for support. The wine had gone right to her head!

With Tyrone helping her, she led the way through to the living-room, where a comfy couch awaited. She pushed him down onto the couch and headed to the kitchen to put the kettle on.

'How d'ya like it?' she called. 'Black or white?'

Tyrone smiled. He caught the double entendre in her question. 'White, please,' he called back.

'You sure you want it white?' Petra answered.

'I'm sure.'

After a couple of minutes, Petra returned carrying two steaming mugs of white coffee. She put them on a side table and plonked herself down on the sofa beside Tyrone. His arm naturally went out around her, and she snuggled into him happily.

'That was an awesome evening,' she said.

'True,' Tyrone replied.

Petra looked up at the handsome man sitting with his arm around her. 'You feeling better now?' she asked, looking up into his face.

Tyrone nodded. 'Loads better.'

Petra studied his face for a moment, then raised her head to kiss him on the lips. They were soft, and after an initial hesitation, he kissed her back. Petra wriggled her body around so that she could kiss him more firmly. She snaked one arm around his neck, and gently kissed his lips. She felt them open, and his tongue gently play around her lips, so she opened her mouth and allowed his tongue to enter it and explore her own.

After a couple of minutes kissing, Petra broke the

embrace.

'Need some air,' she laughed. 'You're an excellent kisser!'

Tyrone smiled at her. 'Thanks,' he said. 'You're not bad yours–'

Petra launched herself on him again and kissed him passionately, cutting off his words. She let her hands roam over his head and around his neck.

Then, with her lips still locked on his, and their tongues engaged in battle, she ran her hand down his chest and to his lap, where she realised she could feel his cock, hard against the material of his trousers.

It was enormous.

Petra allowed her hand to trace what she thought was his length, and it stretched from his crotch part way down one leg! If he had been wearing shorts, then the tip would have been protruding.

Tyrone gasped into her mouth as she gently squeezed his dick with her hand. He was enjoying it!

He allowed one of his hands to move from Petra's neck down to her breasts. He moved his fingers against one of the soft mounds and found that her nipple was hard and erect under her blouse. He gently ran his thumb over the nipple, and enjoyed the way that she squirmed and breathed into his mouth as he did so.

Petra broke away again. 'I'm sorry. I've just got to see this …' She knelt in front of him and smoothed her hands over his trousers, outlining his dick against the material. 'My god!'

Tyrone smiled. 'Ain't had any complaints yet,' he said.

Petra looked up into his face and grinned. She unbuckled his belt and undid the front of his trousers. 'That's gotta be a bit uncomfortable in there …,' she said.

'Let's give it more room, shall we?'

She slid his trousers down, catching and taking his underpants as she went. Tyrone lifted his ass off the sofa to allow her to remove them fully.

As the material was moved down, so more and more of Tyrone's cock was revealed, until it finally popped out, bobbing gently in front of Petra's face.

'Wow!' she mouthed as she took in the massive dick.

She finished helping Tyrone to remove his trousers, then tentatively took his cock in her hand. It was warm and smooth. She tried to get her hand around it, but her fingers wouldn't meet at the other side. She gave it an experimental stroke, allowing the foreskin to move with her hand.

Tyrone smiled and let roll over him the pleasurable sensations of his big cock being played with.

Petra studied the large, purple/black head intently, then placed a kiss on it, before opening her mouth and allowing it to slip between her lips. She teased the little slit at the end with her tongue, and let it move further into her mouth, sucking it as though it was a lollypop.

She let the head pop back out of her mouth, and slurped all up the side of the shaft, licking it. Then she put both hands around the shaft and started to suck rhythmically on the head, her cheeks sucking inwards as she did so. He was so large that she couldn't actually get any more than the head into her mouth, and her pussy was already clenching and getting very wet at the thought of what this impressive weapon could do to her down below.

Tyrone tossed his head from side to side as he was sent into shivers of delight by the attentions of Petra's mouth and tongue, not to mention the gentle stroking that her nails were affording the shaft.

Petra moved one hand down to Tyrone's balls and gently rubbed there, then moved on to his perineum. His balls were heavy with cum, and the shaft so stiff. She noted that it seemed to have grown even more since she started working it.

She removed the head from her mouth and kissed it before standing up before Tyrone. She pulled her blouse off, and her knickers, and stood there stark naked.

He raised his hands to her, and she straddled him on the couch, his enormous dick between her legs and her hands around his neck.

She bent and kissed Tyrone on the lips, their tongues again questing together.

As she did so, she pushed up on her knees, allowing Tyrone's dick to position itself naturally right outside her vagina. She wiggled her hips a little and felt a spasm of pleasure as the head brushed against her sensitive clit.

She tried to sit down on his cock as they kissed, but she was so wet that the head kept slipping out of her vaginal opening and across her bottom instead. Tyrone realised what she was trying to do, and so used his own hand to steady his cock against her opening.

Petra, with her mouth already full of Tyrone's tongue, sank down onto his cock, gasping in pleasure as she felt the invader stretch her lips and start its inexorable path into her body.

She stiffened as more and more of Tyrone's cock seemed to push into her, spreading the walls of her vagina and going deeper and deeper. She stopped moving, feeling that he was in as deep as her body allowed, buried against her cervix, and pulled slowly off him again. She again felt that amazing pulling sensation as her cunt gripped his cock, not wanting him to be gone. Then he was fully out, and she broke the kiss, grinning at Tyrone.

'Not bad, eh?' she whispered. 'I can take it all!'

Tyrone glanced down his body. 'All?'

Petra followed his look and saw the magnificent chocolate-coloured dick standing proud from his body. The tip and some of the length were shiny and wet, coated by Petra's juices, but the bottom four inches or so were still dry. Petra hadn't taken it all after all.

'Oh my God,' she said. 'I've still got that much to go!'

'Looks like it,' said Tyrone.

'I'm not sure ...' said Petra, biting her lip.

'Let me see what I can do,' said Tyrone.

He pushed her away and stood up from the couch, his cock bouncing in the air. He positioned Petra with her face down on the back of the couch, her legs and knees on the seat, and her pussy exposed and facing him.

She held onto the back of the couch and looked back at Tyrone. 'Go gently!'

Tyrone grinned at her. 'I don't think you need to worry,' he said.

Then he grasped her left hip with his left hand, while his right positioned his cock against Petra's pussy once more.

She gasped as she felt the tip enter her, but Tyrone slid only an inch into her, then backed out again. Then he repeated the manoeuvre.

Petra closed her eyes. The sensation was exquisite.

Tyrone slid into her again, an additional inch this time, and then out once more. He continued like this, each time encouraging her forward and then back onto his dick, enjoying the feeling of control that he had over this woman.

Gradually he fed her another inch, and then another ... until he had reached the damp line on his cock from before.

Petra was in heaven. Her pussy was on fire from the working that this magnificent cock was giving her. She had felt a couple of small ripples of orgasm already, and she was so wet, wetter than she had ever been before.

Tyrone kept working her, feeding her more and more of his cock.

She felt a larger tremor coming, and tensed her body as a pre-orgasm rippled through her. She was being fucked by the most magnificent black cock, bigger than she had ever taken before. The thought triggered another small orgasm in her, and she clenched the back of the couch and moaned out loud as it took her.

Tyrone realised that she was rapidly approaching a massive orgasm, and so sped up slightly, giving her more and more of his dick. He could feel her internal muscles clenching and trying to hold him, but failing, and instead he fucked her harder. Holding her hips with both hands, he encouraged her back onto his cock.

With just an inch to go before he was fully embedded in her, the orgasm hit. Petra moaned and then screamed as a massive shockwave of pleasure ripped through her. Her legs shook and her hands clenched the back of the couch as she came all over the cock that was working her so well.

Tyrone didn't stop. He kept his firm thrusting motion going, allowing the final inch of his dick to slide into this willing woman, and sending her wild!

Petra had never felt anything like it. The orgasm just kept on rolling and rolling. No sooner did she think that the waves of pleasure would stop, than another hit her, and then another.

As the massive cock ploughed into her again and again, her eyes rolled back in her head and she gave herself up to the sensations of having the shit fucked out of her.

Tyrone was now pounding her firmly. With his cock now entering to its full length on every stroke, he could let go and thrust into Petra faster and faster. He was like a machine, ramming into her cervix over and over again.

Her juices overflowed onto his cock and made a creamy paste that collected at its base. On each inward thrust she moaned in pleasure; then each time he pulled back, her pussy squelched as the suction caused air to be drawn into her.

Petra was in ecstasy. She had never been fucked so well in her life! She lay there and took everything that Tyrone could give her, as her little pussy spasmed and came over and over again, sending waves of pleasure through her body.

Eventually, Tyrone pulled out and looked down at her, shuddering and moaning on the couch. He wasn't finished with her yet though.

He moved her onto her back, and she lay there, eyes blinking, looking at Tyrone as he loomed over her. She spread her legs for him, and he thrust his dick into her once more, her hole now stretched to receive him. Petra moaned in pleasure as she watched her lover fuck her again, his big black dick vanishing into her little white pussy! She looked down to see her tight cunt clenched and stretched to capacity around his shaft. The pleasure was immense, and she closed her eyes as yet another orgasm wracked her body.

Petra could see why these black guys were so popular. They had stamina and the most amazing dicks!

Tyrone lent over Petra, bracing himself against the sofa, and pounded into her again, faster and faster.

Petra threw her arms around his neck, scrabbling and clutching at his back as he brought her to another rib-cracking orgasm.

She screamed as she came this time, not quite believing that she could cum so much and so often.

Tyrone pulled his dick from her and stood, his manhood bouncing in the air. It was soaking wet, and Petra's cum was matted in the coarse hair at the base.

Tyrone blinked and left the room.

Petra wondered what was happening, as her breathing started to return to normal; but after a moment, Tyrone was there again, his hands rubbing her legs, which were still splayed on the couch. Petra looked down at her pussy, which was red and wide open. She couldn't believe how much cock had just been in there.

'Let's try this,' he said. 'I want to get even deeper.'

Petra grew even more excited at the thought. But how on earth could he get any deeper?

He lifted her knees, then placed his hands under her arse cheeks. Then he pulled her to the edge of the sofa. Keeping her knees back, he parted her legs again, and then kneeled down between them.

He bent his head and began to lick her out. Petra squirmed, her already sensitive clit unable for a moment to take his licking. Then Tyrone pushed her legs back, and he straightened up.

Kneeling between her legs, he had his cock level with her cunt, and Petra looked down her own body and watched with fascination as he eased himself back in. In the few minutes since he'd last been inside, Petra had tightened up again, and her pussy felt every inch of the massive cock as Tyrone pulled back, then rammed himself back into her.

Petra gasped. She couldn't believe it, but with her body positioned at this angle he really was somehow getting even deeper inside her. With each thrust and full penetration he ground his groin into her cunt, and he was soon forcing another climax from her.

'Oh God! Yes. Fuck me!' she screamed.

And he did.

She came once more, and then Tyrone pulled away, encouraging her back onto her hands and knees. Petra moved slowly, her head slightly dizzy from the fucking she had just received. He pushed her down onto the couch and showed her a blindfold that he had obtained from somewhere. *So that was why he left the room*, Petra thought.

Tyrone popped the blindfold onto Petra, and positioned her so that her upper half was on the arm of the sofa while her rear was presented to him further along. He gently rubbed her back and got into position.

'The blindfold intensifies things,' he told her. 'You're going to enjoy this.'

And with that, he held her hips once more, and introduced his dick to her dripping pussy.

She moaned with pleasure as he slid deeply into her, his large cock touching all the right pleasure sensors inside her and making her pussy tremble with orgasmic bliss once more. Petra thought her pussy would never recover from this, but she didn't care. It was worth every second. Even if his cock split her in two.

Blindfolded, she thrust back enthusiastically onto his cock. There was sexual pain, but it was so, so good that she found herself exploding again and again, until she really thought she might faint from the next orgasm.

As Tyrone fucked Petra again, Dave appeared in the doorway.

He saw Petra on the couch, arms resting, body horizontal, ass in the air, and Tyrone behind her, thrusting into her with slow, purposeful strokes.

Dave smiled. All was going to plan. Tyrone had let him into the house as instructed.

He quickly and silently moved a small table to where Petra would have it in her eyeline if she were not wearing the mask. Onto the table he placed a piece of equipment that he often used in his act: a small geared mechanism that spun a disk set vertically into it. The disk was painted with a concentric spiral in black and white, and there were also four small LED lights that blinked at just the right frequency to bypass normal brain function and induce a nice deep trance state.

In order for this to work, the subject had to be deeply relaxed, or otherwise distracted, and Dave was relying on Tyrone to achieve this with Petra.

As if prompted by his thought, Petra moaned and came again, her whole body shuddering with pleasure as Tyrone continued to plough her deeply and firmly.

'Oh, shit, Tyrone,' she said. 'I'm not s-sure ... how ... how much ... more ... oh fuck ... aaaaarrrgggggggg.'

She came again. Hard.

It was nearly time.

Dave set the equipment moving and checked that it was all okay. Then, nodding to Tyrone, who was already looking at the moving spiral, Dave undid the eye-mask and removed it from Petra.

Feeling the mask being removed, Petra smiled. She was in the throes of orgasmic bliss, and as long as Tyrone kept pumping that big cock of his into her, she didn't care what he did.

She opened her eyes, and at first wasn't sure what she was looking at.

The room was dark, but right in front of her eyes was a rotating spiral of white and black, white and black.

She looked and saw that there were also little, twinkling lights all around it, flashing slowly. Red and blue and green and red ...

Tyrone kept fucking her, and she felt another orgasm building inside her.

But what was the spiral? Why ... why ... was ...?

'Oh God oh fuck yes I'm cum – cumming again!'

The huge orgasm hit her, and Petra's body was jerking and spasming again as Tyrone's thrusting started to slow. The device was having an effect on him too.

Petra opened her eyes again, and was immediately drawn into the spiral. She tried to follow it down, but it twisted in her mind and she couldn't. Her eyes just kept following it as the pretty lights blinked and blinked.

When Tyrone finally stopped his fucking motion, both he and Petra were still, staring unblinking at the spiral.

It had done its job.

Dave sat in the lounge at Petra's with a nice fresh cup of tea. He was very pleased with how things had gone. He took a sip and looked at his new toys standing in front of him.

Tyrone and Petra were both still naked, and they stood there with their arms limp at their sides, staring straight ahead, not blinking at all.

Tyrone's dick had softened and was now hanging down once more, and Petra had her juices slowly running down one leg, but both were completely oblivious. Even when Dave had asked Petra to make him a cup of tea she had obeyed without question.

As soon as Petra had become captivated by the wheel, Dave had started taking her down into a deeper hypnotic trance. Her body was so relaxed and her brain so full of endorphins from the expert fucking she had received from Tyrone, that she had been simply unable to resist him. In about five minutes he had had her in a state of deep receptive trance, and ten minutes later, she had become his willing slave.

Dave finished the tea and packed away his equipment, taking care not to leave any evidence that he had been there at all. He even wiped down any surfaces, and the teacup, with a hankie.

Once he was happy that all evidence of his presence had been erased, he turned to Tyrone and Petra.

'Sit,' he said. And both turned and sat on the couch.

'I have some instructions for you,' he said. 'You will listen carefully, and then obey them. Obeying me makes you feel good. You remember that?'

Both nodded their agreement, and Tyrone's cock give a little twitch as he remembered the deeply-implanted instruction that obeying Dave brought pleasure.

'Once I have finished talking, you will wait one minute, and then you will wake, refreshed and happy. You have just had the most amazing sex of your lives. My being here will not be remembered. You will be a little embarrassed at what has happened, but will exchange numbers and promise to keep in touch. Do you understand?'

Both Tyrone and Petra murmured: 'Yes.'

'Excellent. Now, this is what I want you to do.'

When he had finished programming them, Dave was happy. Now he had all his pawns in place.

Anthea was so in love with him that it was insane. She was no longer sleeping with Peter, the Mayor, and had all but barred him from ever touching her again. It wouldn't be long before she demanded a divorce.

Sally was his own little hypno-whore. He had called her several times over the last few weeks, and she had dutifully headed over to his flat, where she had given him head, or fucked him, or just cleaned the place up. Whatever he wanted her to do, she did.

Charlie was also deeply under his control, and was a changed woman. She dressed so amazingly now, and was outgoing and sexy. Dave had let her be, for the moment, allowing her to enjoy her new life, and the men that it brought.

Tyrone was a great subject too; receptive and responsive. He had allowed Dave to get at Petra, and she seemed like a good subject also; very suggestible, and great in bed as well, he noted. He would have to take advantage of that as soon as he could.

But before all that came Nikki and Kym. The last two women who had embarrassed him and made him lose that job ... It amused him to think that Nikki's boyfriend was already his puppet. Soon those last two girls would also be dancing to his tune.

Dave counted Tyrone and Paula down and snapped his fingers. Both their heads flopped, so that their chins rested on their chests. They would wake in a minute's time, and follow all his instructions to the letter.

Dave picked up his bag and, whistling a tuneless jingle, let himself out the front door.

5
Nikki

'A party?' Kym squealed into her phone.

'Yup,' came Nikki's reply. 'And what's more, it's private! So we get to choose what we want to wear, and who gets to come ... and what we get up to!'

'Sounds awesome! When?'

'Friday week.'

Nikki was excited. She'd not been to a party for ages, and Anthea throwing one to celebrate the fact that Peter was finally moving out and giving her a divorce was the best excuse ever! She hoped it would also help to bring Tyrone out of whatever funk he had been in for the last few weeks. She was certainly missing the sex, and was as horny as hell for some action. That was the problem with having a lover as well-endowed as Tyrone: when you weren't getting any, you sure missed it ...

Kym, for her part, just liked to party. Her boyfriend, a lad called Nathan, was a bit cold on anything that involved excesses of drink. He tended to stick to Coke and lemonade, which was fine if she needed a designated driver, but something of a drag for most of the time. She wasn't sure that Nathan was the One anyway ... He was too different from her.

Maybe there'd be someone else for her at the party ... if she could persuade Nikki to let Tyrone bring one of his team-mates with him. Her mouth watered at the thought of one of the six-foot tall basketball lads. All muscles and bulging pants ...

Kym terminated the call and headed back to her office. In her head she was already considering what to wear and how to get Tyrone to bring someone else along for her ... She would put Nathan off ...

Dave had the bottle open and two glasses filled with champagne when his doorbell rang. Right on time.

He opened the door to find Petra standing there. He had a spare evening, and had decided that it was time he tried out his latest conquest. It was always advisable to reinforce his hypnotic control; and he was looking forward to seeing how good she was in bed!

Petra looked a little puzzled. 'Hi,' she said.

'Hello!' said Dave with a broad smile. 'Petra, isn't it? Come in.'

Petra hesitated on the doorstep. 'I'm not sure ... why ...'

Dave took her hand and looked her directly in the eyes. As he looked, he gently squeezed her hand, distracting her mind from what he was saying and sending her into a light trance.

'It's all right, Petra. Everything will be fine. Just listen to my words. You're here about the gym training sessions ...'

Petra gazed into his eyes, and considered that they were very blue. She felt a light fuzziness cross her mind, which quick cleared as she took in his explanation. Of course. The gym. Yes.

She smiled. 'Yes, the gym training. Sorry; it's been a long day!'

Petra entered and Dave took her coat. Underneath she was wearing a figure-hugging pair of leggings printed with a zigzag pattern, and a long T-shirt, cinched at the waist with a metal ring belt that hung loosely at her hips.

Her breasts were round and nice, and brushed the inside of the T-shirt. As Dave had suggested to her, she wore no bra.

Dave ushered her into the lounge and offered her a glass of champagne. Petra took and sipped it.

'Mmmm. Nice. Is there a celebration?'

'Sort of,' said Dave, smiling at Petra.

'Well ... any excuse,' laughed Petra, and downed the rest of the glass.

Dave poured her another and gestured to the easy chair, while he sat on the sofa.

Petra sat down and crossed her legs. 'This is nice,' she said.

Dave leaned across and lit a candle that he had placed on the small occasional table in the middle of the room. It was positioned so that Petra could see it easily. Again, he had suggested to her that she would find the candle fascinating, and he wanted to see how well his instructions had taken.

'So,' said Petra, taking another sip of the champagne. 'About the gym training.'

'Yes indeed,' said Dave, and he started to explain a complicated routine for applying. As he went on, he saw that Petra's eyes kept drifting to the candle. He continued to talk for a moment, then broke off.

'Are you all right, Petra?' he asked.

Petra continued to look at the candle. 'Yes,' she said, in a sort of dreamy voice.

'That's good,' said Dave, slipping into his best hypnotist's voice. 'Do you like the candle, Petra? Can you see it there on the table? Flickering. Can you see it, Petra?'

Petra nodded slowly, her eyes never leaving the flickering candle flame.

Dave could see the light reflected in her eyes.

'Look into the candle flame, Petra,' he said softly. 'Look deeply into the flame. See it flickering and glowing. Look into the flame and let all your thoughts and worries drift away.'

Dave smiled as he saw Petra relax slightly, slumping back into the chair.

'That's good, Petra. You're doing really, really well. Now look into the flame and relax. You want to relax, so take a deep breath in …'

Dave waited until Petra had done as he instructed.

'… and out …

'… and in …

'… and out …'

Petra was an excellent subject. As she breathed according to Dave's instructions, so she relaxed, and as she relaxed, so she opened herself more and more to his direction.

'Now close your eyes, Petra. Close your eyes but keep listening to my voice. You want to keep listening to my voice, Petra.'

Dave's cock gave a twitch as Petra's eyes closed and she settled back still farther into the chair.

'You're happy and relaxed, Petra. Safe here with me. Can you hear my voice?'

'Yessss,' muttered Petra.

'Good, that's really good, Petra. Now I'm going to give you some instructions, and it will make you feel really good to follow them. Following them will make me happy, and making me happy is what makes you happy.'

Petra smiled and nodded. She was ready.

Petra opened her eyes.

She was initially slightly confused as to where she was, but this was quickly followed by the realisation of how horny she was. Her crotch seemed to be on fire. It was one of those deep, deep itches that you know only a good fucking will reach ...

Lucky, then, that her lover and master was there! Petra just knew that the man she was about to service was her master. It was just the way it was. He was an amazing lover of great sensitivity, and his touch drove her wild with desire. She just knew it.

She was standing outside the bedroom door, just waiting for him to summon her.

Petra rubbed her crotch gently through her tight leggings. If she didn't get a good dicking there would be hell to pay!

She heard Dave's voice call, 'Come,' through the door, and swallowed. This was it. This was when she would get laid! She couldn't wait.

Petra pushed open the door and entered the room.

It was dark in there, the only light coming from a bedside lamp that had a red cloth thrown over it.

Dave, her master, was lying on the bed dressed only in a pair of underpants. He looked delicious, and her pussy clenched hard at the sight of him. She couldn't wait to have him!

Petra closed the door behind her and stood by the bed. She needed to please her master, she knew; and she also knew just what he liked!

She slowly reached down and unclipped the metal belt around her waist, letting it fall to the floor.

Then she lifted her T-shirt off over her head, revealing her firm breasts. Her nipples were rock hard, and she let her hands stroke over them, feeling the small nibs pressing against her palms.

Keeping eye contact with her master, she slid the leggings down off her legs, leaving her dressed only in a simple white thong.

She placed one knee on the bed, and started to crawl, as sexily as she could, up to where her master was waiting. She stroked his legs as she went, enjoying the feel of his skin under her hands.

When she reached his crotch, she ran her hands over his bulge, enjoying the feel of the material covering his hard cock. She carefully pulled his underpants down, revealing his proud dick, which bounced gently in the air in front of her face.

She grasped the shaft with her hand, and laid a path of kisses from the base up to the head. Then, with a cheeky look in Dave's face, she swallowed the head of his cock and began slowly sucking it.

Dave shimmied his underpants off his legs and lay back, enjoying the sensation of having his dick expertly sucked by Petra. She rubbed his shaft and stroked his leg as her lips caressed and stroked the head of his dick.

Dave let his own hands run over Petra's back as she sucked at him. It was a glorious feeling.

Petra stopped sucking and rubbing his dick for a moment, and lifted her head.

'Move down,' she said.

Dave scooted down the bed further, so that his head was resting on one of the pillows. Petra moved around so that her knees were straddling Dave's body, her crotch right by his head.

Now he couldn't see her head, but he could feel her hands as they stroked across his pubic hair, and could feel her lips as they found his dick again and started to lick and caress the head.

Dave lifted his hands and moved Petra's thong to one side. This revealed her own sex to him, pink and shaven. Dave extended his tongue and licked gently the full length of her labia, feeling her shudder as he did so. He then moved closer and sucked the hood of her clitoris gently into his mouth, teasing the little nub with his tongue.

In response, he felt his cock slide further into her hot, wet mouth, and her tongue run up and down his length. It was an amazing feeling, made more incredible by the fact that he couldn't see what she was doing.

He concentrated on her clit, flicking his tongue in little circles around it, making Petra moan around the large dick occupying her mouth.

He felt her legs tense, and his cock popped from her mouth as she experienced a small shuddering orgasm from his ministrations. No sooner was that over, however, than her head was back down, sucking on his cock again.

He felt her hands stroke and scratch gently at his balls, and a teasing finger stroke against his asshole. Dave himself shuddered at this. He wasn't sure how to feel about such intimate contact.

Petra wiggled her ass at him, a sure encouragement to keep up what he was doing to her. So, with his tongue again working at her clit, he slid one finger into her vagina and felt it engulfed by hot wetness. She was ready to burst, this girl!

Dave worked his finger in and out, covering it in her juices, then moved it up to her ass, rubbing the slippery fluid around her puckered hole.

In response, she sucked even harder on his cock, and her teasing finger moved deeper, penetrating his ass gently.

It was an amazing feeling. Dave felt simultaneously aroused and scared, as though something was happening that he couldn't quite control.

He pushed with his own finger, and saw Petra's small muscled hole twitch as he sank into it.

She gasped with pleasure, and he gently twisted his finger, giving her the sensation.

Dave felt her finger in his ass move deeper. Then it too twisted, and suddenly Dave felt a deep pressure, the urge to cum, and the most amazing sensations from his dick as Petra sucked at him, slow and steady.

Petra had found Dave's prostate. She had learned this trick a couple of years ago from an ex-boyfriend, but rarely had the opportunity to practise it. She gently rubbed at Dave's sensitive spot – similar to a woman's G-spot, she figured – massaging it and giving him the most amazing sensations. She felt his cock harden further and his balls tighten.

She knew he wouldn't be able to take much more of this, and so readied herself for him to explode.

Dave had to stop pleasuring Petra as his whole groin area became electrified in sensation. Her finger in his ass was doing things to him, and he felt his balls tightening in anticipation of cumming.

He moaned and thrashed his head, and then suddenly felt the familiar pumping sensation as his balls released their load.

Petra felt Dave start to cum, and so clamped her lips

down on his dick as he spurted into her mouth. She sucked and rubbed his cock as he came, milking all his seed into her mouth.

Dave tried to thrash his body, but Petra was holding him down with hers, and when he had finished cumming, she continued to suck him gently.

Dave's cock was super-sensitive now, and he moaned as he felt the sensations overtake him.

'No ... N-no ...' he protested, but Petra was having none of it.

She continued to suck and manipulate his dick, and then suddenly he was cumming again!

A much smaller amount this time, but for Dave, it was the most intense orgasm he had ever had!

He collapsed back on the bed, feeling exhausted and so replete.

Petra finished sucking the cum from him and, licking his dick to make sure it was clean, moved off him.

She grinned at him, and licked her fingers clean of any remaining cum. She had swallowed the lot!

She had done as instructed and made her master very, very happy.

Now she waited for her next instruction, looking adoringly at her master, who was lying on the bed, his cock at half mast now.

Dave looked up at her. She was an excellent little cocksucker. A tremendous addition to his little group.

She looked so sweet and attentive, kneeling beside him on the bed, that Dave took pity on her.

'Lie down beside me,' he said, and Petra did as she was told.

'Now look deep into my eyes. That's right. Deep into my eyes. You're slipping back into my power again, completely into my power and control.'

As he spoke, Petra found herself drawn into his eyes. His amazing eyes. She was totally in thrall to him, and had no thoughts but his. She would do whatever he commanded her to do.

Dave ran his hand over her breasts and stomach, and told her that his touch was orgasmic. That where he touched her, sensations would heighten, and that she would slowly rise to her own orgasm, and cum uncontrollably when he commanded it.

With that command implanted, Dave spent a good five minutes stroking Petra's skin, watching her moan and writhe on the bed.

He raised her little by little until her nipples were again rock hard, and her little pussy was sopping wet and demanding some attention.

Then he stroked his finger down from her forehead, over her nose. Down her chin and neck, down between her breasts and toward her belly button. She shuddered as he circled her belly before moving further down, across her pubis and to her vagina. As his finger touched her clitoral hood, Dave whispered, 'Cum now!', and the first orgasm started, wracking Petra's body and sending her into a shuddering mess. Dave stroked her pussy, letting his finger gently delve into her clenching and shuddering cunt as she came repeatedly.

'Aaaaarrrggghhhhh!' screamed Petra as the multiple orgasms wracked her slim frame, and her hands and legs twitched and try to grasp the bedclothes. She had never had an orgasm this intense. Not even with Tyrone the other week; though up to now, that had certainly been the best fuck she had ever had!

Dave lifted his hand and allowed Petra to come down from the pleasure he had induced.

He instructed her to close her eyes and sleep, and she obeyed, drifting off into a calm sleep, listening to his voice as he helped her to understand more about her body and her thoughts and how things were going to be from now on.

Leaving Petra sleeping, Dave slipped on a dressing-gown and headed downstairs to get himself a glass of water. While he was sipping it, he considered how amazing Petra's reactions had been. She obviously needed a lot of loving to keep her happy, and hadn't been getting much of it lately. Well, he could change that.

To his amazement, his cock twitched and started to return to hardness. The thought of Petra lying on his bed, suppliant and willing, was too much to take!

Ah well, thought Dave. *Can't let a good stiffy go to waste.*

With that, he headed back upstairs, and to Petra. He didn't have to be a psychic to see a good hard fucking in her very near future!

The doorbell rang, and Nikki went to answer it.

At the door was a man she half-recognised. He explained that he had come to see Tyrone about the basketball training.

'Tyrone! It's for you!' she called.

Tyrone emerged from elsewhere in the house and saw Dave. 'Oh, hi man, how's it going?'

'All's fine,' said Dave. 'I just wanted to go over the plans for next week with you.'

'Right. Come in!'

Dave was led into the living room and shown to an armchair, while Tyrone and Nikki sat on the sofa.

'Can I get you anything?' asked Nikki. 'Cup of tea?'

'That would be good,' said Dave, and Nikki headed off to the kitchen to sort out the drinks.

Once they were alone, Dave turned to Tyrone.

'Tyrone. Sleep time.'

Tyrone's eyes flickered and closed. He remained sitting on the couch, but fell instantly into trance.

'Tyrone, when I tell you to return to normal you will remain deeply in trance, but open your eyes and behave as though you are not. Then, you will obey my commands without question. Do you understand?'

Tyrone nodded sleepily. 'Yesssss.'

'Excellent. Open your eyes. Back to normal.'

Tyrone's eyes opened and he stretched. 'Hey boss,' he said.

Nikki returned from the kitchen with the tea, and handed a cup to Dave. 'Here you go.'

'Thanks ... Nikki, isn't it? Tyrone has told me all about you.'

Nikki smiled and shot a look at her boyfriend. 'Has he now. Only good things, I hope.'

Dave considered Nikki over the rim of his teacup. She was an attractive black girl of maybe 23 years old – slightly older than Tyrone. She was wearing a crop top that showed off her flat belly, and her belly button was pierced with a small silver ring.

She wore a tight-fitting pair of denim-pattern jeggings that hugged every curve of her ass and thighs, and her feet were bare, her toenails painted the same pink as her fingernails.

She wasn't wearing too much make-up – she didn't need it – and her hair was frizzy and swept up into a loose bun.

Not bad, he thought.

'Well, he told me some things, Nikki,' Dave began. 'Things about what you get up to ... upstairs ...'

It took Nikki a moment to understand what he was saying, and once she did, her face hardened. 'You mean ... no ... no. He'd never. Tell him Tyrone!'

Tyrone just sat there watching the exchange. Unless Dave gave him a command, he would do nothing. But Nikki didn't realise that. Yet.

'I don't think we need to trouble Tyrone with this, do we, Nikki?' said Dave, adopting his smoothest voice.

'Who are you?' asked Nikki, her eyes narrowing.

'Me? Oh, I'm a hypnotist,' said Dave casually.

'A hypnot ... You're that guy we saw the other month!'

'That's the one,' said Dave. 'The guy you booed and hissed, and got fired ... That guy.'

'I never ... We didn't ... You can't ...'

Dave leaned closer, fixing his eyes on Nikki's. 'I am, Nikki. I am. And you remember that I am rather good, too. Remember what that girl ended up doing during my act? It was all real, you know.'

Nikki shook her head. 'No, can't be.'

'It is, Nikki. And now it's your turn.'

Nikki's face blanched in panic. 'What? You can't. Tyrone! Tyrone!'

She looked at her boyfriend, who was sitting there on the couch, watching the exchange.

'You just going to sit there and do nothing?'

'He's not going to do nothing, are you, Tyrone?' said Dave. 'I think, Tyrone, it would be a good idea if you go and stand in the corner there, and start counting up from one.'

Tyrone immediately stood up from the couch and went to the corner.

'One. Two. Three. Four …' he started to count.

Nikki watched him, astonished. 'How did you do that?' She looked back at Dave, who was smiling at her calmly. 'Tyrone!' she shouted. But he ignored her.

'So, Nikki. I think we should get to know each other a little better,' said Dave.

Nikki shot him a look. 'Not on your life, mister!'

She went to hit him, but Dave caught her arm and held it firmly.

'I don't think so, Nikki,' he said. She looked at him, momentary fear and then confusion crossing her face. 'You see, the way hypnotism works is that you have to want it in the first place. I can't make anyone do anything they don't already want to do, deep down. All I do is release those inhibitions, make the impossible seem possible, make everything seem all right.'

As he spoke, he pulled Nikki to sit on the couch, and sank down next to her.

He looked deeply into her eyes.

'You see, Nikki, even as I speak to you now, and you struggle, you realise that I am more powerful than you. You realise that I will have you, and that you will agree willingly to this, as it is what you want anyway. You want to be taken by a powerful man. Someone strong, who knows exactly what you need. You know that the more you struggle and try to escape, the more you will fall into my eyes. Just look into my eyes. Deep into them. That's right, Nikki. Look deep into my eyes.'

As he spoke, Dave's voice became a gentle crooning that insinuated itself into Nikki's mind. She shook her head to try to loosen the idea, but she could totally understand the logic of what he was saying. She did want to be controlled. To be taken. To have no need to worry.

Nikki moaned and dragged her eyes over to where Tyrone was standing.

'Twenty-nine. Thirty. Thirty-one ...'

'T-Tyrone!' she said.

'Oh, he can't help you,' said Dave, bringing her eyes back to his. 'Only I can help you. Look how easily I controlled your boyfriend, and think how much more easily I can control you.'

Dave felt Nikki starting to relax. His gentle speech pattern was lulling her into the first stages of trance. And of course everything he said was true. He couldn't make anyone do something they didn't really want to. He was playing on the suppressed desires and needs of these people ... even if they didn't realise it themselves.

'Nikki, I'm going to let go of your arm now, but you won't move it. You don't want to move it. You like sitting here listening to me. Looking into my eyes. You know this is right. You know you want to. It makes you feel good.'

Dave released her arm, and it slumped into her lap. Dave could see relaxation starting to play around Nikki's face. Her lips relaxed and opened slightly, and her eyes grew a little unfocused as she continued to stare into Dave's own eyes.

'That's good, Nikki. Excellent. It feels good to relax, doesn't it? Feels good to give me control. Complete control.'

Nikki nodded almost imperceptibly.

Dave smiled to himself and launched into a full hypnotic induction, taking Nikki into trance, eyes open, eyes closed, following each and every one of his instructions. She was a good student, and soon he had her deeply enthralled. Sitting beside him on the couch, eyes open and staring at nothing. Open to his commands.

In the background, Dave could hear Tyrone still counting up like a metronome. This had, of course, helped him immensely. The shock of realising that her big, powerful boyfriend was going to be of no help whatsoever, had weakened Nikki's resolve just enough to allow Dave in through the cracks.

'Now, Nikki,' said Dave.

Nikki turned to look at him. Her eyes wide open, her mind ready.

'I want you to think about this now. You're going to get fucked, here on this couch, by me, right in front of your boyfriend over there. You are going to have the most amazing sex of your life, with a powerful man who controls both your boyfriend and you, and you're going to cum harder than you have ever cum before. Do you understand?'

Nikki was slow to answer. But after considering what Dave had said, she nodded slowly, and Dave noticed a slight smile playing on her lips.

'There's nothing you can do to stop this,' instructed Dave. 'You want this so badly.'

Nikki again nodded, quicker this time.

'So, what is it that you want?' asked Dave.

'I want to be fucked,' said Nikki.

'By whom?'

'By you.'

'How do you want to be fucked?'

'Hard.'

'When do you want to be fucked?'

'Now.'

'So, make it happen.'

At Dave's word, Nikki's face sprang into life. With a lascivious look, she stood and stripped off her crop top, revealing a simple lacy black bra. She reached around behind her and stripped that off too, freeing a nice plump pair of breasts that just demanded to be sucked.

Next to come off were the skin-tight jeggings, and following those her black lacy panties.

She was soon standing naked in front of Dave, and his eyes roamed over her chocolate skin, admiring her curves and sensuality.

Nikki looked down at Dave, still sitting on the sofa. 'Your turn, mister,' she said. 'Get 'em off!'

Dave stood. 'Whatever you say, Nikki.'

He too stripped off his clothing and was soon just as naked as her, his cock standing to attention.

Nikki was entranced by his manhood and fell to her knees, taking it in her hands and then her mouth. Her lips closed around it and she sucked gently, loving the feeling of Dave's skin against hers.

Dave pulled back. He wanted to get straight to the point with this one. He had to assert his full control, and so he pushed her to the floor. She was lying under him, her arms above her head. Dave grabbed a couple of cushions from the sofa. One for under her head, the other to support his knees.

He spread her legs and positioned himself between them. Then, resting on one arm, he moved Nikki's chin so that she was again looking up into his eyes.

'That's it, Nikki. Look deep into my eyes. Look into my eyes and know that I'm going to fuck you now. That you're going to cum, screaming, only when I tell you to. Think about that. And tell me when you're ready for it to happen. Tell me when you want me to fuck you.'

Nikki looked up at Dave. Her master. Her controller. He was so powerful. So in charge. His cock was ready for her. So ready. And she wanted this. Oh my God, she wanted this.

'I ... I'm ready,' she said, looking earnestly into Dave's eyes. 'Fuck me now!'

'As you wish,' said Dave, and at the same time, he allowed his cock to slide between Nikki's pussy lips and up into her wet vagina. *She wasn't joking about being ready*, he thought.

'Oooooohhh,' she moaned as she felt Dave's length enter her. He was so good!

She let her arms fall around his neck as he started to fuck her firmly in and out, his big cock pounding away at her.

Nikki clenched her thighs and tried to keep his dick fully inside her, but she was too wet, and the squelching sounds as she was fucked started to echo around the room, providing a counterpoint to the counting that Tyrone was still providing from the corner.

'Five hundred and thirty-five.'

'Oooohh.'

'Five hundred and thirty-six.'

'Ahhhh!'

'Five hundred and thirty-seven.'

'God!'

'Five hundred and thirty-eight.'

'Yes!'

Dave fucked Nikki expertly in time to Tyrone's counting. The girl was thrashing about beneath him, enjoying the deep fucking she was receiving.

He sped up slightly, wanting to bring her to a peak before he let her cum. She moaned louder and hooked her legs over his, encouraging his dick even deeper into her.

Dave started pistoning hard in and out of her. His cock squelched as it plunged into her hot depths, and her pussy squished in complaint each time the large member was removed prior to another hard thrust in.

Dave could feel that Nikki was ready to cum. She was quivering on the edge of a massive orgasm, which was tickling her pussy and breasts, waiting to explode. But she was unable to reach the plateau.

She opened her eyes, frantically looking up into Dave's. 'Let ... let me cum ... please ...'

Dave grinned at her. His dick was deeply manipulating her now, making small thrusts that would send her over the edge.

'Please ... what?' he asked innocently.

Nikki looked momentarily confused, but then she realised what he wanted. 'Please ... master!' she said.

'Cum now,' said Dave.

And immediately, Nikki started to crest, crying out as the orgasm hit her. She bucked and screamed under him as the most intense sensation of her life rolled over her. It was centred on the magnificent cock that was fucking her so expertly. And of course magnified by Dave's hypnotic commands.

Dave fucked her more slowly as the contractions slowed down and Nikki's breathing started to return to normal.

She closed her eyes, and her muscles went limp. His cock emerged from her satisfied pussy, its job complete.

Dave stood and looked down at the girl lying on the floor. She had been amazing.

'One thousand. One thousand and one.'

'Tyrone, you can stop counting now.'

Tyrone fell silent. Still standing in the corner.

Dave picked up his teacup. The tea was cold. They had been fucking for around 15 minutes ... but then, with hypnotic encouragement, he could get a girl off in less than a minute if he wanted!

And he could always get another cup of tea.

Tyrone and Nikki sat side by side on the couch. Both were relaxed and had their eyes open, staring at nothing. Dave was sitting on the chair beside them, making sure that their trances were good, and that all his control triggers and phrases were locked in place in their minds.

He felt good. Sex with Nikki had been thrilling – Tyrone was lucky to have her! And he looked forward to further sessions with the athletic black girl. But he had one final conquest to make. Kym.

Poor Kym, he thought. She had no idea that every one of her friends was now deeply controlled by him. That they would do whatever he wanted – within certain parameters, of course. What he had said to Nikki was indeed true: you couldn't hypnotise someone to do something that they didn't really want to do anyway ... there had to be some spark of need or want in there in the first place – Dave was just an expert at finding that need and coaxing his secretly willing victims into submission. That was why Anthea had chucked Peter out and was now more or less seeing Dave on a permanent basis. He hadn't had to hypnotise her again for weeks now – she wanted to be with him and to have sex with him ...

Nikki and Tyrone hadn't been getting along. That was why Tyrone had willingly gone with Petra, and why Nikki had given herself to him. Dave had learnt from Nikki that she didn't always enjoy sex with Tyrone, because he was a little too big for her. That was the root of some of their problems. Dave had now fixed it. He had hypnotised Nikki so that she would really enjoy the sex pain. In future, her boyfriend's big cock would always get her off.

Charlie too had wanted a better life, had wanted boyfriends and popularity, and so Dave had provided those things for her.

He really didn't see himself as the bad guy here, even though his original intention had been to make them all pay for what they'd done. Somehow, he had managed to help them all and improve their lives. He couldn't help it. And it would have been bad karma, really, to have done anything else.

And now it was time for Kym.

Dave smiled and gave his final set of instructions to Tyrone and Nikki.

What would Kym's needs be? How would he address them? And what fun would he have when he did!

6
Kym

It was the day of Anthea's party.

She had everything organised. It was to be held at her house, with only her friends and selected others invited. There was a lot of drink available, and she had even laid on some entertainment in the form of Dave the Hypnotist, who would be performing a demonstration for all the guests.

She hadn't told the guests this, of course, as she wanted it to be something of a surprise for everyone. She was actually feeling a little sad at what had happened to Dave at the theatre – her and her friends' behaviour hadn't been very good at all, and since she had got to know Dave better, she realised that deep down he was a decent guy ... At least, that was what she thought ... The fact that he was screwing his way through her friends was something he didn't broadcast ...

Dave waited upstairs as everyone arrived, relaxing with a glass of Coke. He had gathered together all the elements he needed for his erotic hypnosis act ... except that tonight it was going to get more erotic than anyone expected!

Downstairs, Anthea greeted everyone as they arrived, made sure there was music playing and that everyone had drinks. She was the perfect hostess.

She had chosen a little black dress for the occasion. A simple affair, it was little more than a tight tube of black velvet with a slit up the side. It hugged her figure tightly and showed off her prominent breasts to good effect.

First to arrive were Tyrone and Nikki. They seemed happy. Tyrone was wearing his trademark pair of loose jeans, and a smart shirt. Nikki had gone for a glittery dress covered with sequins. She was in party mood, and headed off to choose a drink. Tyrone meanwhile checked out the music system and made sure that the tunes were going to be good and pumping.

Charlie arrived with a male friend. He was a lawyer who drank in the same wine bar that she had visited with Dave, and they were getting on really well. She had opted for a flattering low-cut cat-suit for the party, with a glittering belt that broke up the line and emphasised her small waist. Her date, Howard, had on a business suit, but no tie – this was apparently as casual as he got!

Anthea had just got them settled when Petra arrived. She too had a date with her: another of the basketball team! This was Ashley, a tall white guy from 'up north', as he liked to say. He towered over the petite Petra, who had opted to wear a glittery top over another pair of tight patterned leggings. She giggled as she introduced him. They had been dating for only a week or so, and she was dying to gossip about him with Nikki.

Then Kym arrived. She was on her own as usual, and as usual had not had a good week. She was looking forward to the party, and had made an effort, in that she was wearing a pair of smart trousers and a lightweight blouse. Anthea, however, had predicted that Kym would not have a date, and so had invited a final guest. This was Steve, a chap she had known for some time. Like Kym, he found it really hard to meet anyone he really liked. Anthea knew that Kym and Steve had a lot in common, and so intended to ensure that they got to meet and spend time with each other at the party. She was good at match-making ... it was just a shame that her own life had turned out to be somewhat disjointed in that regard.

The party was a huge success, mainly down to the fact that Anthea kept the drinks flowing, and by the time Dave was due to start his session, everyone was very relaxed indeed.

Petra and Nikki had enjoyed a long conversation in the kitchen about the satisfaction that a nice big cock could bring. Nikki had confirmed that yes, indeed, Tyrone was very well-endowed. Petra had kept quiet about the fact that she knew this, as Tyrone had fucked the life out of her as well, but her eyes had positively shone when she had described Ashley's weapon, and how, when he was fucking her from behind, she literally saw stars!

Anthea assembled chairs in the large dining-room, which had been set up with a makeshift stage at one end, and invited all her guests to sit for the entertainment. She then introduced them all to Dave the Hypnotist, and there was a polite smattering of applause.

Dave felt the strangest of them all, knowing that he was in a room full of people, all but four of whom he had already programmed with deep subliminal commands and could control with just a word. And, indeed, where four out of the five women present he had fucked, with none of them knowing about the others. Well, all that was going to change.

Dave introduced his act, and started his spiel about what hypnotism was and how it worked.

Kym leaned over to Nikki, who was sitting beside her, and hissed: 'Isn't that the same guy from the theatre the other month? The one we thought was rubbish?'

'Yes,' confirmed Nikki. 'Though he's actually pretty good. Just watch.'

Dave asked for a volunteer from the audience, and Anthea stepped forward. Dave spoke to her quietly, and then took her through the briefest of inductions. In fact she had been in trance from the moment he had held her hand, but the others didn't know that.

Once he was happy that he had taken long enough, he introduced Anthea to a broom, and suggested that this was her date for the night ... so she took the broom on a dance through the dining-room, finishing with it cradled in her arms.

Everyone laughed as Dave prised her away from it, and removed the suggestion.

Then he told her that the floor was hot, so she jumped up onto a chair and teetered there for a moment. Next he suggested to her that she was deeply in love with a pop star, who was in fact sitting in the audience.

Anthea targeted poor Howard, and sat in his lap making small talk while stroking his hair. Howard was somewhat embarrassed, but everyone else laughed.

Dave removed that compulsion from Anthea, and then turned to the crowd.

'As this is a private party, we can get a little more risqué than at my normal venues,' he explained. 'As long as we're all adults, and have no problem with adult material?'

There was a chorus of 'No' from the assembled people, and so Dave launched into the next part of his act.

'Many people don't really believe in hypnosis,' he began. 'But that can be easily changed. Hypnosis affects not just the mind, but physical feelings as well. And with physical feelings come physical changes too. For example, you there,' he gestured to Tyrone. 'You look like a nice healthy young man.' He smiled at Nikki. 'And with such a beautiful young lady with you, I'm sure you never have any issue ... getting it up.'

Tyrone blushed. 'What are you getting at?'

'Let me show you,' said Dave. 'Come up front here.'

Tyrone reluctantly headed to the front, cheered on by Nikki and the others.

'Now then. What's your name?' asked Dave.

'Tyrone.'

'Now, Tyrone, I want you to relax and take a deep breath in ... and out...'

Dave took Tyrone through a basic induction as everyone in the room watched. It really didn't take that long as, of course, Tyrone was already deeply under his control.

When he had finished, Tyrone was slumped on a chair, eyes closed, deep in trance.

'Tyrone?' said Dave. 'Can you hear me?'

Tyrone mumbled something.

'I think that was a yes,' grinned Dave. 'Tyrone, it's getting very hot in here. I think you should take off your clothes.'

There was a rustle in the audience as the girls sat forward, eager for a look at Tyrone's body. Nikki had gone on about it, after all. It was only fair that they got a peek.

Tyrone stirred from the chair and started to take his clothes off. When he dropped his trousers and revealed his package to them, Nikki blushed, Petra licked her lips, and Anthea and Charlie drew a breath in pleasure. Although he wasn't hard, Tyrone's cock certainly wasn't small.

'Sit yourself back down there, Tyrone. I'm going to wake you now, and you will feel fine, and not at all embarrassed that you are naked in front of all these good people ... You will also obey all my commands. Okay ... wake up now, Tyrone.'

Tyrone stirred and yawned. He looked out at everyone and smiled.

'So, Tyrone,' said Dave. 'I think that's your girlfriend out there. She looks mighty fine, don't you think?'

Tyrone nodded. Nikki always looked fine.

'I think she's planning on treating you later,' said Dave. 'I bet you know what that means.'

Tyrone grinned, and his cock twitched a little.

'That's right. You're in for a fine time later on. Just look at what your girl is wearing!'

Tyrone's cock grew slightly, uncurling and lengthening.

There was a gasp from the room as it grew to its full size.

'Do I have any volunteers to come and check on this young man's ... *ehem* ... prowess?'

Nikki stood and came to the front. She looked around at her friends. This was her job!

Dave produced a tape measure, and asked Nikki to measure Tyrone.

She set about doing this, and Dave said, 'Tyrone, go flaccid.'

Immediately Tyrone's cock softened in Nikki's hand.

'What's happened? Nikki? Can you do something about that?'

Nikki looked up at Dave. Was this a challenge?

She turned back to Tyrone. 'Come on baby,' she said. 'You can do better than that ...'

She started to caress and rub his softening dick, but nothing she tried made any difference. Tyrone just looked at her, and his dick remained soft.

Nikki glared at Dave. 'You'd better be able to undo this, mister!'

'Of course,' said Dave. 'Tyrone. Stiff.'

At his word, Tyrone's cock started to grow again, becoming larger and stiffer. Nikki held it in her hands and marvelled at the results. He was even bigger than normal, if that was possible.

She rubbed his cock gently, and then used the measure to check his length.

'Ten inches,' she exclaimed proudly. 'That's my boy!'

'Excellent,' said Dave. 'And, of course, this can also work on women.'

He moved over to Nikki. 'Sleep time,' he whispered in her ear, and immediately her eyes glazed over and she fell into his power once more.

Dave made a small show of hypnotising Nikki, even though it wasn't necessary, waving his hands around her face. When he had finished, she was standing in front of everyone, eyes closed and arms limp at her sides.

'Take the dress off your breasts, Nikki,' instructed Dave.

Nikki complied, rolling the top of her sequin dress down and revealing her pert breasts, which heaved a little as she breathed.

Dave gestured to her chest. 'As you can see, at the moment, Nikki here is not aroused. Her nipples are quite flat. But if I suggest that she is aroused ... Nikki, you're getting quite horny, standing up here with me. The sight of your naked boyfriend turns you on ...'

As he spoke, so Nikki's nipples hardened into stiff little peaks, the areola puckering around them.

'Excellent.'

Dave showed her breasts to his small audience.

'I think, Tyrone, that your girlfriend needs a little help here.'

Tyrone pulled himself off the chair and went to Nikki, holding her in his arms, his cock sticking stiffly out from his body. He bent and suckled at her breasts, flicking them with his tongue and making her gasp in pleasure.

'So you see,' said Dave. 'With hypnotism, I can control the physical as well as the mental.'

He looked around at his audience, and noticed that Ashley seemed to be asleep. He went across and checked him, and found that he was actually in a light trance. It must have happened when he was hypnotising Tyrone on stage. Dave remembered then that Ashley had also been in the session he had run at the university ...

Dave grinned at Petra and put his finger to his mouth. Then he took her hand and led her to one side.

'How would you like to have control over Ashley?' he asked.

Petra's eyes widened? 'Really?' she said.

Dave returned to Ashley and, speaking softly in his ear, took him down into a deeper trance.

When he was good and receptive, Dave told him that Petra was a master hypnotist as well, and that he should obey any commands that she gave him. Then he woke him.

Petra giggled. This was going to be fun.

'Ashley,' she said. 'Look at Tyrone there. He's having a lot of fun with Nikki ... I think you could be doing the same with me ...'

Ashley smiled.

'Take off your clothes,' she said.

Ashley stood and took off all his clothes, placing them on his seat. When he was completely naked, Petra stroked his chest.

'Get hard for me.'

Immediately Ashley's dick started to grow, and it hardened and became erect.

Petra grinned at her girlfriends as the full size of his dick became apparent. He was a big boy!

Petra knelt down beside him and kissed the tip. This one was all hers.

As she started to suck on Ashley's cock, Dave turned to the others.

'I did say that this would get quite adult,' he said.

Howard stood up. 'I think it's getting a little late,' he said. 'Perhaps I should be going.'

Dave grinned at him. 'But the party is just getting started. Charlie, you're looking very lovely tonight. I think Howard needs a little attention?'

Charlie looked deeply into Dave's eyes, and her programming kicked in. She all but launched herself at Howard, stripping him of his trousers, and soon he was sitting on one of the chairs, having his cock expertly sucked.

Dave turned his attention to Kym. 'So, how are you enjoying tonight, Kym?' he asked.

Kym giggled. She thought it was all hilarious. 'Loving it,' she said. 'But I bet you can't hypnotise me.'

Dave smiled. 'Do you now. Why do you think that?'

'Well,' she said, 'all this is a trick.'

'Is it? Do you think it's a trick, Steve?'

Steve looked sheepish. Anthea had warned him that things would get quite sexy, and he was no prude. He looked at Kym. She was a pretty girl but had this sort of attitude about her.

'I'm not sure,' he said. 'I'd like to see you try to hypnotise Kym, though.'

Kym shot him a look. 'Go on then. I dare you!'

Dave shrugged. 'Well, if that's the deal. Accepted.'

He led Kym to a chair by the table. Then he obtained one of the candles from the table and lit it.

'Okay, Kym. The first thing about hypnosis is that you have to be quite relaxed.'

Dave noticed that Steve was fascinated by what was happening, so he gestured to him to sit as well. With any luck, he'd be able to take them both into trance at the same time. To help him, he got Anthea to sit with them too.

'Okay, Kym. So, take a deep breath in ... and out ... and in ... and out ... Think about your muscles and relaxing them.'

There was a moan of pleasure from Howard. This was going to be interesting, thought Dave, trying to hypnotise people while an orgy was breaking out around them.

'Look at the candle flame Kym, look at it flickering and dancing there. Try to clear your mind and just focus on the flame.'

Kym was determined not to be hypnotised. She thought it was all a crock, or something everyone pretended anyway. She was a little put out that her friends all seemed to be going along with it, but that was their problem, not hers.

She sat looking at the candle as Dave's voice droned on about focusing on it and concentrating on it.

She was feeling quite mellow. But that was the drink

and the fact that she was sitting down. Nothing to do with getting hypnotised at all.

Her eyes glanced over to where Anthea was sitting. She had the strangest expression on her face. Blank somehow. She was looking wide-eyed at the candle, and seemed to be in some sort of a trance already.

She frowned and kicked Anthea under the table, but there was no response. Nothing.

She looked at Steve, who now had his eyes closed and a slight smile on his face as he followed Dave's words, telling him that he was descending a long flight of stairs, and with each step falling deeper and deeper asleep.

This was a crock, she thought. But she'd better go along with it. She refocused on the candle and on Dave's voice.

In her mind she could see the sea. Gentle waves brushing up on a beach. She was walking on the sand. Could feel it between her toes. And then there was the vast staircase leading down. It was patterned with butterflies and roses, and she could see the individual wings and petals. She could even smell the scent of the roses.

The background noises of moaning and pleasure faded away for her, and all she could hear was Dave's voice gently telling her that everything was all right, that she felt amazing, and that if she just listened to him she would feel much, much better. Because hypnosis was all about feeling great, feeling empowered. No-one could make you do something you didn't really want to. And everyone wanted to feel amazing, didn't they? So, listening to Dave's voice made her feel incredible. And the more she listened, the better she felt.

Dave suggested that she stop to smell the air. She did so, and it was beautiful. She felt a rush of pleasure fill her. Then Dave suggested that obeying him would always make her feel this pleasure. She agreed. It was amazing to obey and feel that rush of sensuality fill her.

She smiled and willingly continued her descent of the steps. One step at a time, each taking her deeper and deeper ...

Dave saw Kym's eyelids flicker and close, the familiar happy smile on her face. He had managed to break through her defences, and now she was well on the way to being his puppet.

Steve too was deep in trance now, and of course Anthea had fallen into trance the moment she had sat down; Dave had conditioned her so well that she was now the perfect assistant for him.

He stopped talking to Kym and Steve for a moment and looked around the room.

On one side, Petra had mounted Ashley. His big cock was pistoning into her little pussy as she rode him. He had a big, happy smile on his face as she threw back her head and came hard all over his dick. Her body shuddered as the pleasure overtook her and she collapsed forward onto him.

Charlie had control of Howard's body now. His cock was deeply embedded in her mouth, and she was pumping it rhythmically, determined to suck the cum from him. He had his hands on her head, and his own head was thrown back in pleasure as she sucked and stroked his dick.

Nikki meanwhile was bent over one of the sideboards, and Tyrone was fucking her from behind. She let out a small squeal each time his massive cock thrust deeply into her. But she showed no signs of the discomfort she'd once had with him. It was all good. And it made Dave's cock twitch to see the sexy black girl getting royally fucked and loving it.

Tyrone grinned at Dave across the room.

'Great party, boss,' he said, and started to fuck Nikki even faster. Her painted nails scrabbled at the polished wood, and her eyes turned upwards in her head as she started to cum all over Tyrone's cock. She was shuddering and crying and moaning all at once, simultaneously wanting Tyrone to stop and to continue fucking her harder and faster, or maybe slower ... She didn't know what the fuck she wanted, but it was so good!

Dave grinned. It seemed that everyone was occupied except himself. Well, that could easily be rectified.

Leaving Steve and Anthea deep in trance, Dave put his hand on Kym's shoulder.

'Kym, listen to me. This is Dave. You're now completely under my command, and you'll do what I say. That will make you feel good. Do you understand, Kym?'

Kym stirred. 'Yesss,' she said, knowing that obeying Dave was actually all she wanted to do.

'Stand up, Kym.'

She stood, eyes closed, like an automaton whose power had been cut.

'Now, Kym, open your eyes and see what your friends are doing. See how obeying me has made them happy.'

Kym opened her eyes and looked around. She saw Nikki enjoying yet another intense orgasm as Tyrone fucked her, slowly now, from behind. Charlie cried out in pleasure as Howard was now eating her pussy out, letting his tongue tease and torment her clitoris. Petra was now on her back, and Ashley was easing his cock into her pussy, one inch at a time, while she moaned and came the whole time.

Kym turned her eyes back to Dave. Her own pussy was now throbbing from seeing all the sexual activity around her.

'I think we could be similarly engaged,' said Dave.

Kym blinked, and knelt down beside him. She licked her lips and undid his trousers. Removing them, she saw Dave's cock crest into view. Then, without hesitation, she plunged her mouth over him.

Dave gasped at the sensation of having his dick sucked into her hot, willing mouth. He grasped hold of the arms of the chair he was sitting on as she proceeded to suck and manipulate him with her tongue. The pleasure was intense. Kym had some seriously good cock-sucking skills!

After a few minutes of this, Dave reached out and held Kym's chin, turning her eyes to look into his.

'Trance Kym,' he said, and her eyes opened wide, staring deeply into his as she fell helplessly into trance.

He took her by the hand and led her out of the room. Everyone else was occupied, except for Steve and Anthea, who were still sitting in trance at the table.

It was time for Dave to enjoy Kym fully, and to complete his revenge over these women.

He led her upstairs to one of the bedrooms. There, with a command from him, she stripped off all her clothes, and all but attacked him on the bed, stroking and caressing his dick, kissing and tonguing it, before moving up his body and kissing him deeply on the lips. She was very desperate to get laid!

Dave pushed her onto her back and positioned his dick just outside her vagina. She spread her legs, holding them open with her hands and arms, and looked pleadingly up into his face.

'Please … please fuck me now!'

Dave needed no further encouragement, and buried his cock in her pussy.

He fucked her comprehensively for about ten minutes. She was orgasming after about five, and thereafter, every movement Dave made gave her tremors and aftershocks. It was as though she had become a little cumming machine, her pussy clenching almost continuously as his cock plunged in and out of her.

Dave pulled out and flipped her over onto her front. She presented her pussy to him doggie-style, and so he took her, fucking her tight little cunt with his big dick until she screamed in orgasm again and collapsed onto the bed.

Dave let his breathing return to normal. That was quite a session!

When he was calm, he returned to Kym, turned her over – she had little strength of her own left – and told her to open her eyes.

She smiled up at him in a sort of bleary way, and then her eyes locked onto his. Dave calmly took her back down into the deep trance that she so desired, and that she had been so adamant she would never succumb to. Then he gave her a series of suggestions and commands that she would find a great deal of pleasure in following. Steve was a nice guy. She would get on well with him, and they would – at least for the moment – have a great time together.

She would also change her attitude toward Dave, and indeed, stop being so angry generally. Dave tried to instil a more positive outlook into her, knowing that positivity bred success more often than not.

Then, with all her programming in place – including some special commands that Dave alone could access – he let her sleep. When she woke, she would feel amazing. Refreshed and in control.

Dave left her and returned downstairs.

In the dining-room, the orgy was continuing. Nikki and Petra had swapped partners now, and were competing with each other to see who could get the lads hard again. The problem for Nikki was that Petra had control over the hypnotised Ashley, so no matter how hard she sucked, teased, nibbled and stroked his dick, it remained resolutely flaccid. This greatly amused Petra, who soon had Tyrone's big cock firmly embedded in her mouth, sucking it and preparing it for her own pussy. Eventually, though, Petra took pity on Nikki, and instructed Ashley that his dick would be the hardest it had ever been. To Nikki's pleasure, the white boy's cock started to grow, and soon was even bigger than Tyrone's. She licked it all over, getting it nice and wet with her saliva.

When both boys were ready, Nikki and Petra grabbed them by the hand and dragged them to the sofa. Then the girls lay back on the couch, their legs spread. A black and white treat for the boys!

Ashley took his position in front of Nikki, while Tyrone stood in front of Petra, and then the boys simultaneously fed the two girls their cocks.

The white dick vanished slowly into Nikki's chocolate brown pussy, while Tyrone's black manhood was swallowed by Petra's little white pussy.

The girls held hands as they were fucked, with their legs raised up and ankles resting on the men's shoulders. The boys took them in unison, fucking slowly at first so that the girls became used to their size, and then faster.

The girls screamed in pleasure, and suddenly Petra squirted all over Tyrone's dick, her legs shaking as she came hard.

Nikki was not far behind, and as Petra's cries of pleasure faded, it was her turn to cum from Ashley's ministrations. She clenched Petra's hand as a massive orgasm took her, shaking her body and causing tears to run from her eyes.

Meanwhile, Charlie was fucking Howard. She was naked, and Dave could see the nipple piercings in her jiggling breasts as she rode her lover. She cried out in pleasure as he played with her breasts and thrust his cock into her. She had turned into quite a free spirit, and Dave was very proud of the work he'd done on her.

Dave headed over to where the drinks were. He needed a stiffener! He poured himself a neat Scotch and added a couple of cubes of ice from the bucket.

Anthea looked so beautiful, he thought; and so far that evening she hadn't had much fun ... Well, he could change that.

Downing the Scotch, he headed over to the table where she was still sitting ...

7
Epilogue

'Cheers!'

The girls around the table all raised their drinks and clinked their glasses together. Then there was silence as they all took a sip.

It was about a week after Anthea's party, and the first time since then that the friends had all got together. Thus it was the first chance they had had to discuss it.

Anthea put down her Martini and looked around at her friends. There had been quite a change in them since the last time they'd enjoyed a girly get together.

Anthea had decided to dress down, and was wearing a tight-fitting purple velvet Juicy tracksuit. She liked it as it was both flattering and very comfortable.

Petra was sitting next to her. She had on a form-fitting top that showed off her lovely cleavage, and a pair of faux-leather leggings that did the same for her ass – especially with the pair of strappy black fuck-me shoes she was wearing.

'How's things with Ashley?' teased Anthea.

Petra's eyes glowed. 'Oh, he's just amazing! So attentive and kind.'

'I told you you'd like him,' said Nikki. 'Tyrone always said he was sad that he didn't have a girlfriend.'

'Well now he does,' said Petra. 'And she's very happy.'

'I know why you're happy,' said Charlie. 'It's because he has such a big cock!'

Petra blushed bright red. 'Well, yes. There are definite advantages in that area.' She gestured at Charlie with her own glass. 'Well what about you, missy? All done up to the nines. I'll never know what made you get that haircut, but it really suits you!'

Charlie grinned. That day, her hair was held in a single ponytail on one side, with the other freshly shaven back to reveal her ear, which sported a very pretty glittering earring. She was wearing one of her favourite outfits too; a black velvet pants suit with a silver belt. It never failed to get admiring glances from every man she passed.

'Howard is lovely,' she said. 'He's a sweet man and treats me right.'

The girls giggled and grinned at each other.

'What about you, Nikki?' asked Kym. 'How are things with Tyrone?'

'We're working them out,' replied Nikki. 'I think they're pretty good, though. He seems to have calmed down a little.'

Nikki toyed with her drink. She was wearing one of her favourite outfits too; a glittery top and a pair of form-fitting jeans. She wondered if she should tell the others that Tyrone had now moved in with her permanently. Perhaps that was news for another day.

'You don't want that man too calm,' grinned Petra. 'I remember at the party ...'

Nikki swiped her hand at Petra. 'True. But then I did

...' she lowered her voice '... give Ashley a good seeing to as well.' She then collapsed into giggles.

'You did, too,' said Petra. 'Poor man couldn't walk for a day!'

Nikki looked at her nails, breathed on them, then rubbed them on her chest. A sign of achievement.

'What about Steve, Kym?' asked Anthea.

'Hmmm,' said Kym. 'Steve ...' She shook her head. 'Too normal for me!' She smiled at the group. 'But it's okay. I met another nice guy yesterday ... and I'm seeing him tomorrow.'

Kym had blossomed since the party. She had used to be a little quiet and sullen, but had now come out of herself and seemed to be enjoying life. Even her choice of outfit for this girly evening spoke volumes: a pair of tight sparkly leggings and a loose, deep-cut silky top that showed off her cleavage to good advantage.

The girls all laughed again, comfortable in themselves and in their relationships. Things were good!

As for Anthea – well, she had got the dead wood well and truly out of her life. Peter had been a boor and a careerist. She'd never tell the others this, but he had hit her on occasion as well. She was glad to have gotten rid of him and grateful to Dave for giving her the opportunity to do so while having some fun!

As far as she was concerned, she had never been hypnotised. Never even been in a trance. She remembered everything, and everything had happened because she had wanted it to. Dave was actually, deep down, a lovely man, and she couldn't now understand why she and the girls had behaved so badly toward him at first. But it had all turned out well.

She suspected that his original motives for contacting them hadn't been that positive. But, despite what they'd done to him, he'd had to follow his own really sweet nature. He had had to help them all. And he had. Everyone had improved and got what they wanted.

She smiled at her friends and raised her glass again.

'Everyone. To Dave!'

They all smiled. 'Yes, to Dave!'

About the Author

Athena Michaels lives in London with her husband John and their two cats Ben and Jerry.

Romance and Erotica From Telos

SINFUL PLEASURES

<u>ATHENA MICHAELS</u>
AWAKENING JESSICA
PIROTICA

<u>ROBERTA STEELE</u>
BYTE ME!

<u>KATE DENNIS</u>
WITCHCRAVEN

ROMANTIC ENCOUNTERS

<u>CATHERINE SERIES BY JULIETTE BENZONI</u>
1: CATHERINE: ONE LOVE IS ENOUGH
2: CATHERINE
3: BELLE CATHERINE (coming soon)
4: CATHERINE: HER GREAT JOURNEY (coming soon)
5: CATHERINE: A TIME FOR LOVE (coming soon)
6: A TRAP FOR CATHERINE (coming soon)
7: CATHERINE: THE LADY OF MONTSALVY (coming soon)

<u>HELEN MCCABE</u>
A GARDEN FAIR
HIGHWAY TO FEAR
HOSTAGE TO LOVE
IN SEARCH OF LOVE
LOVE IN HIDING
THE HOUSE ON THE MOUNTAIN
THE PRICE OF LOVE
WHEN LOVE RIDES OUT